Here are some other Edge Books from Henry Holt you will enjoy:

A Way Out of No Way
Writings About Growing Up
Black in America
edited by Jacqueline Woodson

American Eyes
New Asian-American Short
Stories for Young Adults
edited by Lori M. Carlson

Barrio Streets Carnival Dreams
Three Generations of Latino
Artistry
edited by Lori M. Carlson

Cool Salsa
Bilingual Poems on Growing Up
Latino in the United States
edited by Lori M. Carlson

Damned Strong Love
The True Story of Willi G. and
Stefan K.
by Lutz van Dijk
translated from the German by
Elizabeth D. Crawford

One Bird
by Kyoko Mori

Over the Water
by Maude Casey

The Rebellious Alphabet
by Jorge Diaz
translated from the Spanish by
Geoffrey Fox

The Roller Birds of Rampur
by Indi Rana

Shizuko's Daughter
by Kyoko Mori

The Song of Be
Lesley Beake

Spyglass
An Autobiography
by Hélène Deschamps

We Are Witnesses
The Diaries of Five Teenagers
Who Died in the Holocaust
by Jacob Boas

The
Long
Season
of Rain

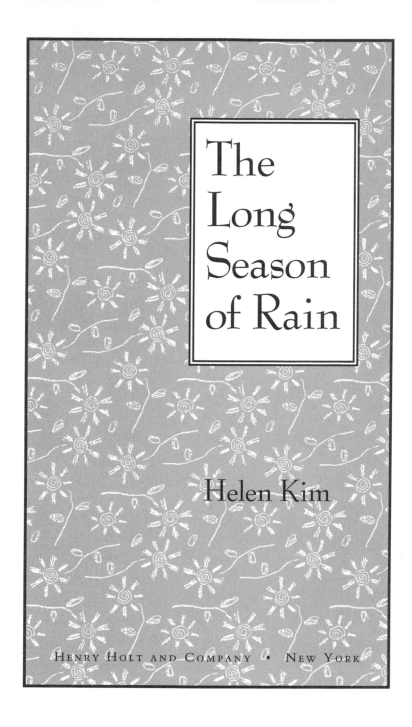

The Long Season of Rain

Helen Kim

HENRY HOLT AND COMPANY · NEW YORK

Henry Holt and Company, Inc.
Publishers since 1866
115 West 18th Street
New York, New York 10011

Henry Holt is a registered
trademark of Henry Holt and Company, Inc.

Library of Congress Cataloging-in-Publication Data
Kim, Helen
    The long season of rain / by Helen Kim.
        p.   cm.—(Edge Books)
    Summary: When an orphan boy comes to live with her family, eleven-year-old Junehee begins to realize that the demands placed on Korean women can destroy their lives.
    [1. Korea (South)—Fiction. 2. Family life—Korea (South)—Fiction.
3. Orphans—Fiction.] I. Title. II. Series.
    PZ7.K55966Lo   1996   [Fic]—dc20   96-16597

ISBN 0-8050-4758-1
First Edition—1996

Printed in the United States of America
on acid-free paper. ∞

10 9 8 7 6 5 4 3

Acknowledgments

I would like to acknowledge and thank the New Jersey State Council on the Arts for the prose grant, the Wesleyan Writers' Conference for the Jacobson Scholarship, the Stonecoast Writers' Conference for the Delogu Scholarship, and The Virginia Center for the Creative Arts for a residency.

Many have supported me throughout the writing of this novel. I would like especially to thank Mona Simpson for her generosity and guidance, and Denise Gess for her belief in my novel and advice. To Ketrin Saud and Eric Kim, I am ever grateful for their unwavering faith and love. I owe many other thanks to my agent, Irene Skolnick; my editor, Marc Aronson; and all my friends who took part in this journey, including Hamlet.

*For my parents
and for Marina, Lucy, and Rosa*

*for those moments when we knew
what love was*

—H. K.

Contents

The
Long
Season
of Rain

PART I

The
Rain

 # The Boy

When the unbearable heat and high humidity in Seoul made the dark clouds billow so that we could almost hear the static in the air, we called it an electricity day. On those days in late June everything seemed restless. Our dog whimpered, then barked for no reason, and sparrows fluttered around the yard. We felt uneasy until the lightning struck and the first heavy drops hit the ground. Then *changma*, the long season of rain, began.

On the first days of *changma*, Grandmother would sit in the living area and slowly fan herself. As she surveyed the yard, she mused over the damage the rain could bring us that year. Grandmother was always calculating, if not the cost of the roof tiles and gutters during *changma*, then the price of newly harvested rice in autumn. From time to time, she would stop fanning and count something with her fingers until a worried look came over her.

The rain usually continued for three to four weeks with brief breaks until everything in the house—clothes, food, papered walls, and even the wooden floors—soaked up the dampness. A moldly smell drifted and surrounded us constantly, and everywhere our bare skin touched felt sticky.

My sisters and I sat side by side and watched the yard through the thick lines of rain. The rose petals drooped heavily, pushed toward the ground by the pelting drops, and the earth that couldn't soak up any more water spat out mud. The patter of rain hitting the marble steps harmonized with the softer sounds that came as it fell on the earth.

With not much else to do, we waited for and welcomed any visitor who came by. We liked hearing the local news and sometimes even more important national news about *changma*. Every so often a community perched on the mountain slid down from the deluge and everyone and everything were buried. We could not quite visualize houses sliding down the mountains, pigs and cows swimming, or people drowning in rain.

But in the summer of 1969, during a particularly long and bad *changma*, we met one of its victims. We were bored from playing jacks all day and the sight of Grandmother Boksoon, one of our grandmother's church friends, perked us up. We sat with Grandmother and the guest, waiting for Mother to bring in a plateful of fresh peaches and grapes. But when Grandmother started to pray, as she did with all her guests, her friend began to cry and Grandmother shooed us out of the room.

Changhee Uhnni, my older sister, and I sat close to

the rice-paper sliding doors and tried to listen to what the guest was saying. Our younger sisters just watched us. Grandmother Boksoon said that her daughter, son-in-law, and grandchildren were sleeping when part of a mountain slid down and buried their house. No one survived except for one grandson who dug his way out. Crying, she said that she couldn't afford to keep this grandson because she was too poor. She wanted to know how God could make her so poor and make this happen to her too.

The shuffle of Mother's feet chased us away from the doors, but we put our heads close to them again when she went inside. That was when we heard Grandmother make an arrangement with Mother to have the orphaned boy stay with us until a home could be found for him.

We put on our rubber slippers and pattered outside to the storage room. Moonhee and Keehee, our younger sisters, followed us into the dark room full of rice sacks, rice sifters, crates, rusted pots and pans, tools, and ceramic jars. Changhee Uhnni turned on the light by pulling a string and then sat on a rice sack. We squatted on the floor and waited for her to speak first because at thirteen she was the oldest. We added the term "Uhnni" to her name as we did to almost all unmarried older females. Two years younger than my sister, I could comment from time to time, but Moonhee, nine, and Keehee, six, mostly listened and asked questions.

"Did you hear that?" Changhee Uhnni asked, towering over us.

"I know—a boy is going to stay with us," I said excitedly.

"What boy?" Moonhee asked with the lisping sound she had been making ever since she lost her two front teeth.

"Grandmother Boksoon's grandson," Changhee Uhnni answered. "Don't you remember? He came here once."

Moonhee shook her head. I also didn't remember seeing him.

"How old is he?" I asked.

"Ten or eleven," Changhee Uhnni answered.

"He's my age," I said.

"Maybe, but he is younger than I am, so he better behave." Changhee Uhnni was the same with our younger cousins. She bossed them around whenever she could.

"What's he going to do here? We don't have any boys' toys or anything." I had seen trucks and tanks, soldiers and guns, at my boy cousins' house.

"How do I know? He just better not touch my things," Changhee Uhnni said.

"Where is he going to sleep?" Moonhee asked.

"Maybe he can sleep with Grandmother," I said, looking at Moonhee.

We were delighted. No one ever wanted to sleep with Grandmother because she asked too many questions and smelled like geraniums, her favorite flowers. Every night Mother would ask one of us to sleep with Grandmother, and when no one answered, she picked Moonhee, who protested the least. Besides, Moonhee was Grandmother's favorite. The rest of us slept with Mother and Father in the big room across from Grandmother's room, which was joined by the living area.

"I like that. Let the boy sleep with Grandmother."
Moonhee smiled.

"He can sleep with Soonja Uhnni," Changhee
Uhnni said.

"But he is our guest!" I said.

"He's from a poor family, an orphan. He can sleep
with the helper."

Changhee Uhnni was always saying things like that.
Once she made Soonja Uhnni, who is six years older
than she is, cry by telling her that she came from the
lowest class in all of Korea. Mother made us call Soonja
Uhnni a helper, not a maid or servant. Mother said we
should treat her like one of the family.

We heard Mother's voice, muffled by the sound of
rain. She came into the storage room.

"I told you there are mice here. You shouldn't have
brought your sisters here," Mother said to Changhee
Uhnni.

"How long is the boy staying with us, Mother?"
Moonhee asked.

"You should not have been listening." Mother turned
to Changhee Uhnni, who was scowling at Moonhee. Then she said to Moonhee, "Grandmother will
decide that."

Mother picked up Keehee, brushed the dirt off her
legs, and held her to her cheek.

Keehee is a boy's name, as is my name, Junehee. They
named us when we were still in our mother's womb
because they thought the names would make us boys.
We asked why it was just Keehee and me, and Mother
said after Changhee Uhnni was born, our relatives said
to try a boy's name for me. After I was born they just

believed the third child, which was going to be the last, would be a boy. Then Mother tried one more time and named the youngest Keehee.

The boy arrived a couple of days later, when our father was still away. Father often went to America in his work as a colonel in the army. It was just as well; he didn't like strangers.

The boy came with Grandmother Boksoon, who was wiping her eyes with one hand and hugging the boy's head to her side with the other. The boy was so skinny that his eyes looked large and his ears stuck out. He wore ugly brown shorts and a gray shirt, and his sneakers were ripped on the sides. The square gauze taped on his knees was soiled and even his neck looked dirty. When Grandmother Boksoon left, Mother brought the boy to the kitchen and closed the door to wash him. She only closed the kitchen door in summer for privacy.

Soonja Uhnni came into the big room where we had been waiting for Mother to come in with the boy. She went through the cabinet drawers.

"What are you looking for?" I asked.

"Some clothes for the boy."

"He can't wear girls' clothes," Changhee Uhnni said.

"Mother said to bring them."

"Don't touch mine," Changhee Uhnni warned.

"Don't worry," Soonja Uhnni said and took my gray shorts, white-and-blue-striped shirt, and my underwear with small pink flowers.

A little while later Mother came in with the boy. We

couldn't stop giggling even though Mother gave us a warning look with her eyes. Mother had double-fold eyelids like Westerners, and when she looked up, her eyes sunk in a little, which made them scary.

The boy looked all right in my shirt and shorts, which were baggy on him, but we knew he had on girls' underwear and that made us giggle.

"This is Pyungsoo. Pyungsoo, Changhee is the oldest. Junehee is your age, Moonhee and Keehee are younger than you."

The boy didn't lift his head but stood next to our mother as if he were being punished.

Mother took out the medicine box from the cabinet drawer and started to nurse his wounds. He had badly scraped knees and elbows, and parts of his arms and legs had black-and-blue marks. On one side of his face he had several cuts near the temple. Mother put Mercurochrome on his wounds and taped white squares of gauze over them, telling him the whole time it wouldn't hurt him. Still the boy held his breath until the red liquid dried.

Mother called Soonja Uhnni and asked her to get some ice cream, a special treat.

"Do you know what ice cream is?" Changhee Uhnni asked in her mocking tone.

"Of course he does," Mother answered for the boy, and smiled with her eyes.

Then Changhee Uhnni asked, "What grade are you in, anyway?"

When the boy didn't answer Mother asked him gently.

"Fourth," he said.

"What school do you go to?" Changhee Uhnni continued.

The boy looked at Mother and Mother nodded.

"Booksung," he answered.

"That's a cheap public school on the other side of the mountain, isn't it?"

"Changhee," Mother cautioned her.

Grandmother slid the wooden doors open and peered in. "Pyungsoo looks clean," she said. "Maybe tomorrow Changhee's Mother can get him some clothes from the market."

"Yes," Mother said and sat up a little, smoothing her skirt.

Grandmother came in, and Mother looked for a straw mat and pushed it in front of Grandmother.

"I don't need this, don't worry," Grandmother said, but she sat on the mat anyway.

"Let's see." Grandmother took the boy's hand and examined his palm lines, then let it go. "Not much fortune according to those lines. Do you remember how you got out?" Grandmother asked loudly, as if the boy were deaf.

The boy shook his head.

"Were you all sleeping in the same room?"

The boy nodded.

"It's a miracle, then, that you got out." After a pause Grandmother continued, "I was there once. No, that shack couldn't hold in this rain. It was too high up on the mountain, with a weak foundation. No, it couldn't hold." Grandmother clucked her tongue. "Losing everyone like that. Your mother should have married better."

The boy frowned.

"I told Soonja to get some ice cream," Mother interrupted.

"Good. The boy needs something. The way he looks, skinny and dark, reminds me of Jungmin when he was young."

Once in a while Grandmother called our father by his name. Most of the time she referred to him as "the children's father."

"When did he say he was coming back?" Grandmother asked Mother.

"In about a week," Mother answered politely.

"Hm . . . we probably won't be able to find a home for the boy by then."

Soonja Uhnni came back with the ice cream and Grandmother left, saying it was too creamy for her. I watched the boy eating slowly and squinting his eyes when it got too cold in his mouth.

Grandmother decided that the boy would sleep with her. All of us lay side by side on the bedding with the colorful blankets Mother had laid out on the floor for us. Moonhee, who usually slept with Grandmother, was happy to be next to me. After Mother turned off the light and left to finish her work, we tried to be quiet but it was no use.

"He is wearing a girl's panty." Changhee Uhnni's head went under the blanket like a turtle's.

Moonhee crawled to my bedding. We pulled the blanket over our heads and tried to muffle the sound by cupping our mouths with our hands.

"I didn't see, Junehee Uhnni," Moonhee whispered. "Which pair was it?"

"One with the small pink flowers." I felt sorry for the boy but still couldn't stop thinking how silly he might look.

"Don't they need the kind with the hole in the front?" Moonhee asked in her shy voice.

"Shhh, you are not supposed to know things like that."

"Sungjin Opa wears those—I saw it." Sungjin was a cousin of ours who was older than Moonhee. She called him "Opa," which is used for older male relatives and friends. Even though he was ten years old, sometimes he ran around just in his underwear.

We squealed.

"Shhh!" our youngest sister Keehee warned us. "Mother said no more talking."

"Poor boy," Moonhee sighed.

"Why? Because he has to sleep with Grandmother?" I whispered.

"No, because he has to wear your underwear." We started to giggle again and tears formed in our eyes.

"Be quiet! You are going to get me in trouble," Changhee Uhnni said.

"Uhnni laughed too," I said.

"Don't do it anymore. Mother will come back."

That made us be quiet, but it was too late. Mother had an extra eye and ear. She could hear us from any part of the house and see what we did when she wasn't around. We heard the double wooden doors slide.

We fell silent.

"No more talking, I said. You know Grandmother has to wake up early. Moonhee, go back to your place."

Moonhee crawled to her bedding.

Grandmother went to her Methodist church every morning at five o'clock. She often complained of not sleeping well.

After Mother closed the door and left, I held Moonhee's hand and tried to sleep, wondering if Grandmother held the boy's hand with her thin fingers. None of us liked it when she did that. She had dry skin with liver spots.

In the middle of the night I was awakened by a piercing sound. Mother, who slept next to Keehee, got up quickly and rushed to Grandmother's room. She came back with the boy in her arms. His breathing was loud and uneven, and his body shook in Mother's arms. Mother stroked his face, which was cradled in her breasts, and rocked him like a baby. Slowly the boy stopped shaking and his breathing calmed down.

Changhee Uhnni and Moonhee stirred without really waking up, but I couldn't sleep for a while. I listened to the boy's breathing and watched Mother, who was bent over him, whispering.

CHAPTER 2

 Five Stone Jacks

We were playing jacks with five small stones in the entryway to our house, sheltered from the rain and away from Grandmother. She didn't like us playing jacks in the living area because the stones made marks on the wooden floor, but more so because we were noisy when we played. As all traditional houses in Korea, our house had very little privacy. If we wanted to play loudly or talk away from adults' ears, we had to move away from the main section where the living area joined Grand-mother's room and our big room that we shared with Mother and Father.

The wooden lattice sliding doors covered with rice paper in Grandmother's room and our room didn't keep much noise out. We could hear Grandmother reading the Bible in her room with all the doors closed or the telephone conversation in the living area, even if Mother or Grandmother was whispering. We learned to read each other's lips when we didn't want the adults to hear us, and we always tried to play quietly.

More than anyone else, though, Mother knew how to do everything quietly. She could open her clothing cabinet door or slide out her dresser drawer almost without a sound. When she needed to talk to Father, she waited until night and then spoke softly. If she wanted to be alone, she went to the vegetable garden through the little door in the surrounding wall. Sometimes we found her there even in the middle of the winter, when the thickest socks barely kept us warm inside.

We lived in a typical Korean house, though our vegetable garden was not that common. The house was in the shape of a horseshoe, and in the hollow middle was a courtyard with a rose garden where white, pink, and red roses bloomed in early summer. Facing the garden from the living area, the left arm had the kitchen, the pantry/dining room, and our helper's room. The right arm included the storage room, the entrance area, the bathroom, and an extra bedroom that became Changhee Uhnni's and mine that summer.

Except for the main section, where we could go from our bedroom to Grandmother's without putting on shoes, the other parts of the house were not internally connected. When it rained, we had to put on our shoes and walk underneath the eaves in order to go to the kitchen or the bathroom.

The house and the grounds were surrounded by a protective wall. All that could be seen from the street was the gray tiled roof that sloped down, turned up in the corners, and jutted out from the main structure.

During *changma*, spurts of water gushed from the jade-colored gutter that ran along the tiled roof.

"Pyungsoo." Mother put her hand on the boy's shoulder. "Go play with Junehee." She pushed him gently toward me, but the boy didn't budge.

Since the boy had arrived two days before, he spent most of his time standing by the open kitchen door and watching our mother. He followed her wherever she went. We tried to include him in the things we did, but he just shook his head and looked for our mother. When he needed something, like a glass of water or a piece of paper, he tugged on our mother's skirt.

"You can't follow me around all the time," Mother said to Pyungsoo. "Go and play, then we'll eat ice cream later."

He shook his head again. His hair was long and covered most of his eyes. Still, he looked much better than he had when he arrived. The black-and-blue marks had turned yellow, and the scrapes were turning into scabs. Mother bought him two shirts and shorts, underwear, new sneakers with a cartoon drawn in the front, and *komooshin*, traditional footwear made of white rubber. *Komooshin* were handy during *changma* because the mud washed off easily.

When Mother nodded and pushed him gently, the boy looked at her wistfully and followed me slowly.

"Sit here." I pointed to the spot next to me.

He squatted between Moonhee and me. Changhee Uhnni gave him the once-over with her mean eyes.

"It's your turn," she said to me.

"Can't we show him how to play first?"

"It's your turn. We are on the fourth one. Jacks are for girls, not boys."

"Mother said to play with him. Besides, we taught Sungjin how to play."

"He's our cousin."

"Mother said . . ."

"Yes, yes." Changhee Uhnni was annoyed. "Here— here is how you do it." Changhee Uhnni took the stones and began to go through the rules very quickly. Pyungsoo just stared at her.

"You got that?" she said when she was done. "We'll start over. Moonhee and I are on one team, and you and Pyungsoo, on the other," she said to me.

Keehee, who hadn't learned to play yet, just watched us.

"You start." Changhee Uhnni gave the stones to the boy.

Changhee Uhnni was never fair, and if we told her that, she would say, "So, I get blamed first for everything. Do you think that's fair?"

Pyungsoo took the stones and to our surprise got it right, tossing one stone in the air and picking up the others one at a time. The tiny curls in the corners of Changhee Uhnni's mouth disappeared.

She was next, then me, then Moonhee. When it was Pyungsoo's turn again, he did his with ease. We got all the way to the fourth sequence and Changhee Uhnni missed a stone. Then it was Pyungsoo's turn.

He threw one stone up high and quickly grabbed the four on the ground. But as he caught the falling stone, one dribbled off his hand.

"Hah! You missed it!" Changhee Uhnni said.

"No, he didn't," I said. "He dropped it after he finished."

"Nope. Give them to me."

"Let him do it over, please." She let our cousin do that once in a while under very special circumstances.

"Nope." She made up her mind, but Pyungsoo didn't budge. He just sat with the stones in his hand.

"Give them to me," Changhee Uhnni insisted. When he sat there without moving, she poked his arm with her index finger.

"Leave him alone," I said.

Pyungsoo didn't retaliate. He just sat there until she poked him so hard he fell on his behind. That made Changhee Uhnni laugh loudly.

The boy slowly pulled himself to a standing position.

"Give me the stones." Changhee Uhnni put out her hand and the boy threw the stones at her. Most of them hit her arm, but we heard the *tock* sound of one hitting her skull.

"*Ya!*" Changhee Uhnni screamed. "Stupid idiot."

She stood up, put her hands on her hips, and glared at him from the corners of her eyes with her face turned a little away from him. The way she did that was just like Father. Her features weren't as sharp as Father's, but the long, narrow eyes and the thin, defined lips made her look as mean as him, especially under her straight bangs.

She muttered, "Stupid orphan, who does he think he is . . ."

"What's going on?" Mother stepped in. The kitchen

was straight across the yard from the entrance area and Mother could see everything.

"That, that stupid orphan"—Changhee Uhnni couldn't get her words out fast enough—"hit me with the stones. Look, Mother." She showed her arm but there were hardly any marks.

"You should never call him an orphan again."

"But he threw the stones for no reason."

"Did you hear me? Don't ever call him 'orphan' again."

"Yes, Mother." She withdrew her arm.

"Why did you throw the stones?" Mother asked, putting her arms around his shoulders. Pyungsoo didn't answer.

"Changhee, you have to be very patient with him."

"I let him play with us and everything." Changhee Uhnni didn't take her eyes off him. "You should punish him."

"Changhee, he is younger than you. You have to be thoughtful, more than usual." Mother always spoke to her as though she were usually thoughtful.

"I was."

"Okay, then try harder."

"He hit me! Why is Mother on his side?" she demanded.

"I'm not on his side."

"Yes, you are. I didn't do anything wrong. Look." She stuck out her arm one more time.

"I'm not going to punish him."

Changhee Uhnni breathed through her teeth. "You are nice to him because he is a boy."

"No, because he is our guest."

"No, because you wish you had a son!" Changhee Uhnni blurted out, but then I saw how sorry she was by the way she bit her lip.

Mother stared at her hard with her deep-set eyes. "When you are this mean and spiteful, I wonder if you came out of me at all."

"Who else could I be from?"

"From your father's blood," Mother said in a low, controlled voice.

After a few seconds of complete silence, Changhee Uhnni burst out crying. She turned around, opened the front door, and ran down the stairs to the street.

It was still raining hard.

Mother sighed and hit her chest a couple of times with her fist. The boy, who was standing next to her, ran across the yard and went into our helper's room.

The rest of the afternoon we read, waiting for the front door to creak. It wasn't the first time Changhee Uhnni had run out of the house, but it was the first time she didn't come home for an entire afternoon. The last time was when Father slapped her on the head because she didn't want to share her children's magazine with us. Even though she had bought it with her money, Father called her selfish and a bad example for the rest of us.

By the time Grandmother came home from her outing and sat down to dinner, Changhee Uhnni hadn't returned.

"Where is Changhee?" Grandmother asked.

"She wasn't getting along with the boy. I scolded her," Mother answered. "She ran out of the house."

"Ran out of the house? In this rain?" Grandmother studied Mother's face carefully, then us. "Well? What happened?"

"We were playing jacks with the boy," I volunteered.

"Playing jacks? With the boy?" I hated the way Grandmother repeated words when she asked questions.

"Yes, Grandmother."

"And? Was Changhee losing?"

"Yes, Grandmother."

"And?"

"And the boy threw the stones at her," I said quietly, trying not to look at him. "Changhee Uhnni was mean to him first."

"That's why she ran out of the house?"

"I scolded her," Mother said, but still Grandmother stared at Mother. "Severely."

That seemed to satisfy Grandmother. She said, "Always the firstborn, they are the most jealous. Let's eat. Where can she go?"

We ate in silence. We could hear the clinking of the spoons and the silver chopsticks against the bowls. But the silence was broken when the boy, who had been hunched over the table picking at a few dishes, began to cry out loud.

Finally, when it got dark, Mother sent out Soonja Uhnni to look for Changhee Uhnni, and we soon heard them come in. Changhee Uhnni was soaking wet and shivering. Mother gave her dry clothes to change into and set up a dinner table in the pantry/dining room, where Soonja Uhnni ate after us. We heard the murmur of Mother's voice and Changhee Uhnni answering, "Yes, yes."

When Changhee Uhnni came into our room, her eyes were puffy and her hair was still wet.

"That stupid orphan, he is going to get us in a lot of trouble. None of you better be nice to him. If you are"—she pointed at me—"I'll tell Mother about your math test."

Changhee Uhnni, who never got less than a 98 in any subject, kept track of my grades. She found out about a math test I didn't bring home.

"You understand? All of you?" She asked.

I nodded, and Moonhee and Keehee followed.

The next day at breakfast, Changhee Uhnni wiped her chopsticks when they accidentally struck Pyung-soo's while reaching for the fish, and she didn't say one word to him the whole day. All of us avoided the boy, and he followed Mother around; she finally gave him a book and said if he read it, she would give him ten won. He sat in the living area and looked up every few lines to see where Mother was. We were all relieved when Grandmother took him with her to one of her church functions that evening.

CHAPTER 3

 Auntie Yunekyung

Auntie Yunekyung, Father's older sister, visited us the next day. It was still raining and she carried a red umbrella with a scalloped edge. She plopped down in the living area with her feet still out on the stone step. Changhee Uhnni, who was practicing the piano, and the rest of us got up to bow.

"Mother, I'm here," Auntie called out after receiving our bows.

Grandmother came out of her room.

"Where is Changhee's Mother?" Auntie asked.

That's what everyone called our mother. Never Junehee's Mother or Moonhee's Mother or Keehee's Mother, but always Changhee's Mother, just because she was the oldest.

"She went to the market," Grandmother answered. It was almost dinnertime and Mother had gone out to pick up some groceries.

"In this rain?" Then Auntie called out, "Soonja, bring me a bucket of water."

"Where are your boys?" That was the first question Grandmother asked whenever she saw her daughter.

"Getting tutored, and Sungjin is at his friend's." Auntie had three sons. The older cousins were studying for their entrance exams, one for the university, the other for high school. The youngest cousin, Sungjin, went to the same school as us.

"Did you finish your work around the house?" That was the next question Grandmother asked.

"Yes."

"Where did you get that tacky umbrella?"

"At Myungdong," Auntie answered curtly.

"Isn't it enough that you dress in red? Do you have to carry a red umbrella? Do you know how old you are? Your sons will have wives in a few years."

"Don't start, Mother," Auntie said in her annoying, high-pitched voice. "You shouldn't tell a forty-two-year-old woman how to dress or what color umbrella to carry, or what makeup to put on, for that matter."

Grandmother clucked her tongue but didn't say anything more. She always yelled at Auntie about her appearance, but she was also particular about her own clothes and wore the brightest lipstick of all the grandmothers we knew.

Soonja Uhnni brought the water and Auntie poured it gingerly on her delicate white feet, rubbing away the mud. Then she dried them and came into the living area.

"Where is the orphan?" Auntie asked, looking around.

"With Changhee's Mother," Grandmother said.

We hadn't been very friendly to the boy because Changhee Uhnni watched us like a hawk, and when she caught me handing a book to the boy, she threatened to tell Mother about the math test again and about the twenty won I spent on street food.

"What are you going to do with him?" Auntie said, adjusting her jade ring and looking at her hand.

"Find him a home, if anyone can feed another mouth at this time."

"Why not keep him here?"

"Here?"

"Like a houseboy—he could probably help out." Auntie was rubbing away a mark on her fingernail.

"I can't keep my friend's grandson as a servant."

"I'm sure Grandmother Boksoon doesn't expect the boy to do better."

"She doesn't expect her grandson to become a house-boy. Besides, he's too young."

"Who knows? When all the girls leave, maybe he could take care of Jungmin and their mother," Auntie said.

"We won't leave!" I said. "We'll stay here forever."

"Of course you'll leave." Auntie smiled, showing her red lipstick smudged on her teeth. "If you don't get married and leave, you'll be a burden to your parents."

"We won't get married." Moonhee joined in.

"Well, that's what you say now, but you'll change. You'll see. Besides, your father may like the idea of having a houseboy," Auntie said, and I saw from the corner of my eyes Changhee Uhnni shutting her book.

"Don't be ridiculous," Grandmother said.

"Why?"

"Even a houseboy has to be fed and clad. Besides, you know how your brother feels about . . ."

We heard the front door creak. Mother and the boy came in. As soon as Mother saw Auntie, she bowed stiffly and told Pyungsoo to bow too. Mother asked Auntie whether Soonja Uhnni had served her tea. When Auntie said it was too close to dinner-time, Mother went to the kitchen. Pyungsoo followed behind.

"Come here," Auntie said in her singsong voice.

The boy halted and came slowly toward us with his arms dangling by his sides.

"Go wash your feet first," Grandmother said, and when he went to the kitchen, she whispered to Auntie, "Don't say anything about the boy staying here in front of their mother."

"Why not?"

"I don't want her to get any ideas." Grandmother then turned to see if we heard her. Adults always did that. They talked in front of us as though we were either deaf or stupid.

When the boy returned, Auntie made him sit in front of her and asked him questions.

I put on my rubber slippers and went to the kitchen. Mother was bent over, peeling a cucumber.

"Mother," I called, and she turned around. "What are we having for dinner?"

"Fish. Why? Are you hungry? Do you want some fruit?"

I shook my head. "Is Auntie staying for dinner?"

"Why don't you ask her to stay?" Mother went back to peeling.

"Doesn't she have to go home?"

"She can do as she pleases." Mother smiled bitterly.

While our mother rarely went out except to the market and church, and once in a great while to her mother's or her best friend's, Auntie was hardly home. If she wasn't visiting her friends or cousins, she was over at our house, especially when something was going on, like Grandmother's birthday dinner or a gathering.

Then Auntie sat with the guests in her red dress and laughed and talked while Mother went back and forth with a tray. On these occasions, Auntie loved to sing for the guests. At first she would decline, but when they insisted—and they always did—she would clear her voice, a sure sign of giving in. Then, with her hands gathered by her breasts, she swung side to side and sang in her soprano voice that sounded a little like a bird trilling.

Mother never complained or said one small bad thing about Auntie, even if Auntie's husband did. Once, Uncle came over and protested to our grandmother that his wife was rarely home. To that Grandmother said, "What makes you think she will listen to me when she doesn't listen to you, her husband?"

Then another time he complained that his wife didn't know how to dress for her age. Uncle tried to buy gifts of brown, beige, and other modest-colored clothes for Auntie, but Mother ended up wearing them. Auntie would come over with those clothes and say to our mother, "He knows I don't wear these colors. Do you want them?" Mother would say, "I can wear any color." Then she took out the waist and the arm holes and expanded them.

Mother didn't have half as many clothes as Auntie. She had her house clothes, which she wore at home, and dressy clothes, which were mostly given to her by Auntie. Mother didn't put on makeup when she was home, and if she went out, it was never bright red.

When dinner was ready, everyone sat around the table. Even without Father the table was cramped with Auntie and the boy.

"Here, have some fish." Auntie put a piece on the boy's rice bowl. He played with the fish for a while, then looked at Mother.

"You don't have to eat it if you don't want to," Mother said.

The boy put his fish on Mother's rice bowl. That's what we did when we didn't want to eat something. We put it on her bowl when Father wasn't watching.

"It's good for you—it's delicious," Auntie said. "Isn't this a nice place?"

Pyungsoo nodded.

"Your house was so small. I don't know how all of you—"

"Auntie, try some seaweed soup," Mother interrupted. "It's very good for the rainy season."

Auntie said, "Yes," but she went on talking to the boy. "Tomorrow you come over to my house. I have a son your age. He has lots of toys."

The boy didn't answer her, but Mother said she would send the boy with me.

That night, as every night since Pyungsoo came, he had a nightmare. After the first night, Mother let him sleep with her in our room so he wouldn't disturb Grandmother. Unfortunately Moonhee had to be sent back to Grandmother's room. In the middle of the night, Pyungsoo screamed and whimpered like a dog, with his arms and legs shaking. Even when he took naps in the afternoons, he sweat and woke up wide-eyed and looked at us as if he didn't know who we were.

CHAPTER 4

To Auntie's

It was raining hard the next day, and although the walk to Auntie's house took only ten minutes, Mother made us put on our rain gear. The boy wore my raincoat and I wore Changhee Uhnni's, since she didn't want to lend him hers. On our feet we had on *komooshin* because when the rain came down slanted, as it did on that day, our rain boots were no good, and the rubber shoes were easy to wash off. The boy's *komooshin* looked like rowboats and mine were narrower, like canoes. When we were ready, Mother gave me twenty won and said to buy ice cream or candy for the boy and me.

From our street we turned right on the main street and walked in the direction of the mountain behind our neighborhood. We passed the rice shop full of square rice sacks, the general store that sold everything from vegetables to brooms, and a Realtor where two old men with long beards sat smoking. Past that was the

pharmacy, and next to it was Dr. Pae's office, where we
went for various sicknesses. We turned right at Dr. Pae's
office.

The hilly side road to Auntie's house was narrow,
lined with walls fencing in the houses. Vines of roses and
morning glories cascaded from these walls, drooping
heavily. The boy and I tried to avoid small ditches where
muddy water rose and swirled sometimes to our ankles.
Our feet squished as we walked along.

The boy didn't say anything and didn't stay too close
to me, so I held the umbrella near him and tried to
think of something to say.

"Our cousins are all boys. The oldest one is eighteen,
the middle one, fourteen, and the youngest, Sungjin, is
ten. He'll be there." The boy still didn't say anything.
"We are on our recess now, but Sungjin and I go to the
same school, down that way." I turned and pointed
toward our school. He looked.

Close up I could see thin blue veins showing under
his eyes and the fresh white skin where the scabs came
off on the side of his face. They reminded me that he
had lost his entire family in one night.

"Changhee Uhnni is mean to our cousins too," I said.

That made the boy look into my eyes.

"My sisters' names are Kyungja"—he spoke slowly—
"and Myungja and Shinja. That way." He pointed to
our left. "I know which way I came from. That's where
we lived."

It was hard to tell where he was pointing because
beyond the mountains were many other towns.

.   .   .

"So, that's the orphan," Auntie's helper said when she opened the door.

I didn't much like their helper. She was young and rude, not like our helper, who only sounded gruff but was warm inside.

"Your aunt will be back soon." She barred the door behind us.

We walked in, and already our bratty cousin Sungjin stood in the living area looking the boy over.

"Who's that?" Sungjin asked.

"Pyungsoo," I said. I was afraid that Sungjin would make Pyungsoo cry, as he often did us.

"Here," Sungjin extended a toy soldier to Pyungsoo when we went into the living area. Pyungsoo hesitated. "Here, go ahead," Sungjin said again, but when the boy tried to take it, Sungjin pulled his hand back quickly. Then he offered the toy soldier to Pyungsoo again. "Really, you can have it now. I was just joking before." But Sungjin did the same thing, this time grinning. "You can't touch my toys, not any of them, ha-ha-ha."

"Sungjin, give him the toy, please," I asked nicely.

"You can play with it," he said to me, "but he can't touch my things." Sungjin circled around the living area with the soldier making a machine-gun sound. *Tu-tu-tu-tu-tu-tu-tu.*

"Please, Sungjin," I pleaded.

"You want to come into my room? You can, but he has to stay out here."

I shook my head. Sungjin continued to make a lot of noise, having his toy soldiers fight one another, and glancing at us with his awful grin.

None of us liked Sungjin. Whenever he came over to our house he caused too much trouble. If he wasn't climbing onto the roof and jumping down, he was playing with our father's lighter or a box of matches. One time he set a large box of matches on fire in the room and scorched the ceiling. Grandmother was always yelling at him, and he called her names we would never even think of: Devil Granny, Stingy Granny, Monster Granny.

But what we hated the most was when he tried to kiss us. Moonhee and I were his favorite victims, and we had to hide in the closet or the attic or behind our dog Star's house, even though it was dirty there. He always found us and against our protests kissed our faces, then threatened to kiss us in school if we told on him. Afterward we had to run to the water faucet and wash off all traces of his lips.

The only time we were glad to see him was when he and our father got into a boxing or wrestling match. Father would knock down our cousin every time, count to ten, and announce his triumph by raising his arms and walking around the room. Then they started another round. We liked seeing Sungjin lose badly, and we tried to learn boxing from Father. At first he said it wasn't for girls, but then he put out his hands, palms facing us. We punched his hands as hard as we could but Father just smiled. We were no match for Sungjin.

Auntie Yunekyung returned with a bag of goodies for us: a box of Haitai cookies, fruit-flavored candies, and my favorite pastries, with white cream between the pancake-shaped layers. Sungjin was nicer to Pyungsoo when she was around. We munched on the sweets.

Auntie took out a piece of paper.

"When is your birthday?"

"May first," Pyungsoo answered.

"What year?"

"Nineteen fifty-eight."

"Let's see. That's dog year, isn't it?"

Pyungsoo nodded.

"What time were you born?"

"I don't know," he answered politely.

"Are you sure you don't know what time?"

Pyungsoo shook his head.

"You don't even know whether it was morning or evening?"

He shook his head again.

Auntie frowned and tapped on the wooden floor with her long fingernails. "I won't be able to look up your fortune, then. We won't be able to tell if you are suitable for their family." Auntie sounded disappointed. She liked going to fortune-tellers.

When we were done eating, Auntie ordered Sungjin to play nicely with Pyungsoo and added that if he didn't, she wouldn't buy him a fire truck. Sungjin gave the red plastic soldier to Pyungsoo and told him it was a North Korean soldier. Soon the boy who hadn't said more than a few words since he came to our house was making the same gun noise, *tu-tu-tu-tu-tu-tu-tu,* rapidly pushing around the toy tank and the toy soldier to fight Sungjin's good South Korean soldier.

Auntie and I sat in front of her makeup bureau.

"You have beautiful skin, just like me. It's your best feature," Auntie said while powdering my face. She put some red lipstick on my lips and spread it evenly with her pinkie.

"Rub your lips together like this," she said. I copied her and dabbed my lips with a white tissue she handed me.

"Junehee, what do you think of having a brother?"

"A brother?"

In the mirror, I saw how different Auntie—with her almond-shaped eyes and button nose on a round moon face—was from me. My eyes drooped, and I had Mother's full lips, which stuck out a little because of my buck teeth. Mine was a plain face, but when Auntie dusted the powder and put lipstick on me I looked more like her.

"What brother?" I asked.

Instead of answering me, Auntie hung back and cocked her head to get a good look at my face. She twisted her lipstick out, dabbed it on each of my cheeks, and spread it with her fourth finger; then she powdered my face again. The smell of the powder reminded me of fresh flowers.

"Don't you wish you had a brother?"

"Not really," I said.

"Sometimes I worry about your mother and father."

Auntie was erasing something from the corner of my mouth.

"Your mother isn't as lucky as me," Auntie sighed. "You look almost pretty," she said, and I did look almost pretty in the mirror.

Out of the four of us, Moonhee had the prettiest

face, with her shining black eyes and cherry-colored lips. Next came Changhee Uhnni, with features like Father, Keehee, with Mother's full lips but more shapely and Father's eyes but kinder, then me.

"You want your nails done too?"

I nodded even though I knew Mother would clean them as soon as I got home. I liked how Auntie made my nails come alive by brushing on bright red. When Auntie was finished with my nails, she told me to spread them out and not touch anything. Then she took my hairband out, brushed my hair, rebraided it, and tied on one of her polka-dotted ribbons.

"You want to be my daughter?"

I just smiled. Auntie said if she had a daughter, the daughter would be beautiful. She said it was a shame that no daughter could take after her, with her white skin and pretty face.

We heard a loud cry, and Auntie and I rushed out to the living area. Pyungsoo was crying, and it seemed like Sungjin was about to kick him.

"What did you do this time?" Auntie demanded.

"He didn't give back my tank," Sungjin complained.

Pyungsoo was holding his left arm. Auntie rubbed his arm and hit Sungjin on the head. She took away the plastic tank and gave it to Pyungsoo, but he didn't want it.

"What did I say?" Auntie yelled at Sungjin. "I said to play with him nicely. Didn't I tell you this morning he was an orphan?"

I went and sat next to the boy and waited for him to stop crying. Auntie brought in a towel and cleaned his face. She offered him the tank to take home, but the boy refused and cried louder, kicking out his feet on the floor. After trying to console him for a while, Auntie thought maybe he would feel better if we left. We put on our rain gear and started for home.

CHAPTER 5

The Toy Soldier

Pyungsoo refused to walk with me under the umbrella, even though he could hardly open his eyes from the rain pelting his face. Every time I edged closer to him, he moved away. I gave up and walked behind him, trying to rub off the makeup. My palm was smeared with lipstick, and the nail polish that wasn't completely dry speckled and streaked. I didn't bother with the umbrella anymore and let the rain wash my face. When Pyungsoo got to the bottom of the hill, he glanced back, then waited for me.

"Is my face clean?" I asked, and he shook his head.

I took off the polka-dotted ribbon and cleaned my face with it, then shoved it in my pocket.

This time when I opened the umbrella, Pyungsoo stayed under it.

"Sungjin doesn't know how to share," I offered.

"I had toys before, lots of them," Pyungsoo said

proudly. Then he didn't say any more and we walked in silence. When we were almost home, I remembered the twenty won.

"Want to stop by the shop? I have the money Mother gave me."

Pyungsoo nodded and we headed for the stationery shop. Mr. Moon's stationery shop was past our house on the main street between a small general store and the uniform shop. We didn't like Mr. Moon, who only smiled at us when we went there with Mother or Grandmother. But it was the only neighborhood shop that had school stuff, toys, and ice cream.

The store wasn't lit very well, and on rainy days it was hard to see where everything was. I shook the water off the umbrella and put it against the ice box, where the ice cream was kept, but I didn't think Pyungsoo would want ice cream just then. Instead, I went by the toy section, where little plastic stars, shovels, kettles, and other colorful knickknacks were displayed.

"Go ahead, pick what you want," I told him. First he was hesitant, then he leaned closely when he saw a green plastic toy soldier.

"How much is that?" I asked Mr. Moon.

"Seventy won," he said, looking over the glasses hanging on his nose. I could tell he didn't like the way we were dripping onto his things.

"You have to pick something else. I only have twenty won," I said.

"Items on the right side are twenty won," Mr. Moon said from behind the counter.

Pyungsoo leaned over, looked for a long time, and picked out a plastic orange shovel, and I paid Mr. Moon.

As I reached for the umbrella I heard a shriek. When I turned around Mr. Moon was holding the boy's arm, and in the boy's hand was the green toy soldier. He was twisting to get away from Mr. Moon.

"You little thief, you didn't think I could see. You . . ." Mr. Moon's chin quivered. "I'm going to teach you a lesson you'll never forget. You bad boy." Mr. Moon slapped the boy's head repeatedly.

"Mr. Moon, Mr. Moon!" I screamed frantically. "It was my mistake, my mistake." His hand stopped in midair. Then he looked at me with his mean little eyes.

"Your fault? Well, who is this boy? I know your parents wouldn't let you have friends who steal."

"Maybe he thought he could have the toy soldier too for that money. He's . . . he's . . . he's an orphan."

"An orphan? That's why he is stealing. Orphans steal all the time. No one teaches them anything."

"No, he had parents, but they are not here anymore."

"Well, where are they? I'm not going to let him go until they come and pay me."

Pyungsoo's shoulders heaved. He was sobbing again.

"They passed away in a *changma* accident. That's why he is staying with us."

Mr. Moon let the boy's hand go, fixed his glasses, and said, "Well, I'm going to let the boy go with the toy, but tell your mother to come down and pay for it. I'm not going to tell the police or anything since he had a misfortune, but she has to come down and pay for it."

I was afraid to say we couldn't take the toy soldier because I knew Mr. Moon would get angry again. So I shoved the toy soldier in the boy's pocket, took his hand, picked up the umbrella, and left the shop quickly. He was still sobbing and refused to get under the umbrella.

We couldn't go home the way things were, so I began to walk down the main street. I couldn't think of any-place to go except my school; there we found a dry spot by the entrance to the building. We sat on the steps.

"Why did you take the toy soldier? Don't you know that you can't take anything without paying for it? Mr. Moon said Mother has to pay now. She only gave us twenty won," I yelled at him.

The boy took out the soldier from his pocket and threw it in a puddle, and then threw the shovel in the opposite direction. They both floated on the water.

"I don't want the toy soldier, I don't want the shovel, I don't want anything. I just want to go home." He put his head on his knees and began to cry.

I couldn't say anything to him because I knew he didn't have a home anymore, and I couldn't say he could stay with us. I just sat there and thought about how I could pay Mr. Moon that seventy won without telling Mother or anyone else.

Mother wouldn't mind it so much but she would have to tell Grandmother, who would surely take back the toy soldier. Besides, if Changhee Uhnni found out about it, she would get upset about the boy's new toy. When the boy stopped crying, I picked up the toys and gave them to him. He shook his head, but when I offered them again he shoved them in his pockets.

"Don't tell anybody about the toys," I told him as we headed home.

"You can play with them if you want."

"Okay, but we can't show them to anybody, especially the toy soldier."

When we arrived home, Mother asked me why we were both soaking wet. I told her about what our cousin did to Pyungsoo, and she didn't ask any more questions. She told me to go wash my face with soap and clean off the nail polish. Then she dried Pyungsoo's hair.

At dinner Pyungsoo seemed a little more cheerful even though he didn't say much, and he ate most of his food.

The only person I could think of asking for that money was our helper, Soonja Uhnni, but she didn't always keep our secrets. After dinner, when Mother was laying out our bedding and blankets, I went to the kitchen. Soonja Uhnni was busy cleaning the floor.

"What do you want?" she asked brusquely.

Soonja Uhnni was from the south and had a heavy accent that made her sound almost quarrelsome. She said that where she came from, a village so deep in the mountains that she had to walk half a day from the train station, everyone spoke like her. I felt sorry for her because she was only sixteen when she had to leave her father and come up to Seoul looking for a job as a servant.

"Can you lend me seventy won?"

"Why? What are you going to do with it?" She was always busy doing something and hardly looked at me when I spoke.

"I can't tell you, Uhnni, but I will pay you back little by little."

"Why don't you ask your mother?" She sprinkled a little water to make sure the dirt would not rise and then swept the floor vigorously.

"I can't ask her. Please, Uhnni."

"What are you going to do with the money?"

"Nothing bad."

"Did Sungjin threaten you when you were over there?" She meant did he try to kiss me.

"No, it doesn't have anything to do with him."

"All right, I'll give you the money, but you'll have to pay me back. I'm saving to go home someday." She hadn't gone back home for three years. She just sent money to her sick father.

I followed her to her room, which was small and damp. She opened her suitcase, took out a bundle, and untied the knot. Inside the wad of cloth was a smaller package wrapped in newspaper, and she unfolded that. The money was wrapped in tissue paper. She counted the bills carefully and gave them to me.

"If you don't give this money back, I'll have to get it from your grandmother."

"Don't worry, I will." When we came out of the room, I wanted to hold her hand, but she was already heading to the kitchen. Besides, she would ask me what I was doing.

Mr. Moon was very happy when I gave him the money. He even asked how the boy was. I knew he didn't care about the boy at all. He was just glad that he could get his money. For every non-school book we read we received ten won from our mother. I would have to read seven books for the toy soldier, but it was worth it because the boy became a little more friendly toward us and didn't follow our mother around so much.

Still, he avoided Changhee Uhnni, who let him know his place mostly by ignoring him. I just waited for the rain to stop so we could get out of the house and go to the school playground or to the nearby mountain.

 The Surprise

On the day of Father's return, Mother got up early. While Grandmother went to her church in the morning, she went to the Dongwon bath house, stopped by the beauty parlor, and changed to a fresh skirt and blouse when she returned. Normally Mother went to the bath house on weekends with us, but on that day she wasn't doing anything in her usual way. In the afternoon, she went to the market to pick up some meat and vegetables for a stew. When we asked to tag along she said, "Not today, I have too much on my mind."

Grandmother too was getting ready, inspecting our room and the rest of the house. Even though Soonja Uhnni had polished the furniture the day before, Grandmother took a soft cloth and gingerly rubbed her brown lacquer cabinet set that was inlaid with mother-of-pearl, and Mother's red set in the big room.

Grandmother also polished the piano, the wooden chest in the living area where the phone sat, and even the clock on the wall. Then she dusted the bedroom wallpaper with its shiny green leaf design and took down all the picture frames to be cleaned.

While Grandmother went back and forth from the big room to her room, she counted with her fingers the days Father had been away. It was the third of August. The rain should have stopped completely by now, but it hadn't, and the ground was soft and soggy.

The more everyone bustled around, the more nervous Pyungsoo became. He sat alone in our helper's room and played with the toy soldier.

"Mother wants you to come wash and change clothes," I said after we put on new clothes in the afternoon.

"Why? I already washed this morning."

"She wants you to do it again."

Pyungsoo got up reluctantly and followed me, but I knew even if he looked his best it wouldn't make any difference to our father.

We hardly saw our father except at breakfasts. He worked six days a week as an instructor at the Military Academy and often went away to different countries to attend conferences. When he did come home early enough for us to greet him and have dinner with him, he seemed tired and expressionless.

At breakfast Grandmother often asked, "Where were you last night?"

Father answered, "With my colleagues."

"Were you drinking again?"

Sometimes he answered, "Yes," and Grandmother finished the sentence with, "Come home early tonight. The children never see you anymore."

But when Father was in a bad mood he said, "I'm a grown man with four children—don't tell me what to do."

Grandmother sighed and didn't say anything after that, but she was at it again the next morning.

We were mostly silent when Father ate with us, and we watched what we ate. Changhee Uhnni and I were the right weight, Father said, but Moonhee was too skinny and Keehee was too chubby. When Moonhee didn't want to finish her bowl of rice, Father made her do it even though she had a stomachache afterward, and Father didn't allow Keehee a second bowl of rice. He said all girls have to watch their weight, and that this was done in the advanced countries like America. But when Father was not around, all of us ate what we wanted.

After breakfast, Father put on his khaki-colored uniform with three round brass emblems on each shoulder that were like the circle in our flag, divided in the middle with a wavy line. He looked at himself in the mirror, turning to one side and then to the other, pulling down his jacket and sticking out his chest. That made him appear a little taller than his average height. Then he put on the cap, pulled in his chin, and corrected the visor several times until it sat on his head perfectly straight. While he did this, his mouth was closed tightly and we could see the muscles flex on the sides of his face.

Our adult relatives frequently talked about how handsome our father was. They said when he was young he looked just like Montgomery Clift and women flocked to him. Even though we didn't know this American actor, we assumed he was as handsome as our father. Father had perfectly groomed dark eyebrows, not too thick or thin, long almond-shaped eyes that seemed either too delicate or too sharp, and a mouth that had precise expressions.

Some people used the word "pretty" to describe our father, but by the way his mouth tightened around the corners, we knew he didn't like that description. Father seemed too calm to get angry, but we knew that at any moment his eyes could become triangles and the rest of his face, steel.

When he was in a good mood, after fixing his uniform he sang in front of the mirror with hand gestures like the singers on television. He sang some adult songs we didn't understand, something about a woman's black gloves, or life coming and going, or the last leaf dangling from a branch. Sometimes he sang in English.

Mother said that when Father was training at the Military Academy, he learned English quickly and had the best pronunciation in his department. Father was always asked to speak and translate whenever high-level officials came from America. Every time he sang in English, we quieted down and listened to his pronunciation and watched his tongue rolling and twisting to make the strange noises. Even though we didn't understand him, we recognized the melody. He said it was titled "Secret Love."

Once in a while after he sang, he acted like a clown.

He made a scrunched-up face and said, "Chigi chigi chaga chaga," while walking around the room like a hunchback. We laughed at him because he was trying to make us laugh. Afterward he went out to a waiting jeep that took him away until nighttime.

On Sundays when he was home, and if he wanted to speak to us, he said loudly, "Gather at my room in five minutes." We had to stop whatever we were doing and go to him. He made us stand in front of him in a row and said, "At ease."

We put our hands behind our backs and stood with our feet apart.

One Sunday he said, "You need to exercise. Every morning you will do ten minutes of calisthenics."

He repeated the movements several times, bending down, twisting, and stretching, and even showed us a waist exercise that was good for girls. Then he told Changhee Uhnni to lead us.

"Understand?"

"Yes, Father," we answered.

Then he said, "Dismissed." That meant for us to move away to somewhere else.

The next morning Changhee Uhnni led us to the yard, and we giggled throughout the whole routine, except when we thought Father was watching us—then we became serious. Keehee could hardly follow any movements and at one point fell on the ground. We laughed at her.

At first we did the exercises because they were silly and funny. But after a few days Changhee Uhnni didn't ask us to come out to the yard, and no one complained. A few more days passed and we completely forgot about calisthenics. One morning during break-fast, Father asked Changhee Uhnni whether she had been leading us in doing what he had ordered. Father knew she hadn't because he had been there every morning.

Changhee Uhnni stammered, "Well, we did a little bit and then . . . Mother didn't remind me . . ."

"It's your responsibility to lead your younger sisters, not your mother's!"

Father made Changhee Uhnni stand in the yard with her arms straight up in the air, and yelled at her every time her arms came down a little bit, "Get your arms up this instant!"

Grandmother, the only person who could tell Father what to do, said, "She is just a child. I think she will exercise from now on. Changhee, tell your father you will exercise."

"Didn't you want me to educate my children?" Father glared at her.

Grandmother didn't say anything after that. Mother, who was in the kitchen, first pretended she didn't see anything, then she left the house with her market bag even though she didn't usually go shopping at that time. We sat with Grandmother and helplessly watched Changhee Uhnni cry and twist her body under her falling arms.

When Father left for work, Changhee Uhnni just crouched in the yard and cried out loud. Mother, who returned with an empty basket, told her to go wash her face and get ready for school. Mother said to all of us that Father didn't ask us to do too many things but when he asked, we had to obey him. She reminded us every morning to exercise after that, but Father didn't pay attention to us anymore until the next time he was in a bad mood, and then he punished us in meaner ways.

All day Grandmother, Mother, and I looked toward the front door, and finally it opened and the sergeant driver came in with Father's bags. Mother rushed out from the kitchen, took Father's smaller bag from his hand, and carried it into the living area. Father bowed to Grandmother, nodded and acknowledged us, noted the boy with his eyes, and without a word handed his cap to Mother, who was standing next to him. Then he went into the big room, and Mother hung his cap on the hook on the wall and went back to the kitchen.

"The flight was too long. It took over thirty hours," Father said after taking his jacket off. "When is dinner ready? I had to go without *kimchee* for two weeks."

"Soonja!" Grandmother called out. "Bring in dinner as soon as it's ready."

While Father changed into a comfortable cotton shirt and shorts, we gathered around Grandmother and watched her take out his clothes from the bag and separate the ones to be washed. Then she took out a watch, Coty face powders and jars of face cream, chocolates, medicine, a scarf, and some fabric. We loved to look at these presents Father brought back from his trips.

"Mother," he said, "pick out what you want and decide which ones need to be given away."

Grandmother always had the first pick, then Auntie, then it was our mother. But often before Mother got anything, Grandmother said there were relatives and friends who knew of Father's trip and had to be given something.

"Is this everything?" Grandmother turned the bag inside out and shiny things fell out of the side pocket. They were little sequined coin purses in different shapes and colors.

"They're for the children," he said quietly.

Once in a great while, Father really surprised us. He never gave us gifts when we expected them, like on our birthdays or Children's Day, but then he would surprise us. That was how we knew he didn't forget us completely. Changhee Uhnni picked a strawberry-shaped one, then I picked a fish, Moonhee, a grape, and Keehee, a bird. Mother ran out of the kitchen to see what we were squealing about.

"Father brought you gifts!" She smiled widely, her eyes happy with wrinkles. "Did you thank Father?"

"Thank you," we said in unison.

Grandmother, seeing that Pyungsoo was left out, gave him a bar of chocolate. Father looked at Grandmother questioningly.

"He is Grandmother Boksoon's grandson," was all she said, and Father didn't pay much attention.

We compared our little purses and looked through the catalog Father brought back. The glossy pages had women with yellow hair in flips posing in girdles and

brassieres. We giggled and looked through some more.
There were clothes, shoes, machines, and many other
things we had never seen. Father said that it was the
most popular catalog in America, Sears.

We sat around the dinner table too excited to eat
even though there was a delicious meat stew. Mother
had brought out the large table and set it on the floor.
There would have been no room for Pyungsoo at our
regular table. As Father munched on *kimchee* he talked
about the weather in Texas. He said that the weather was
so hot and humid, it was worse than going through
changma in Korea.

Mother didn't say very much but rearranged the side
dishes from time to time so that the best dishes were in
front of Father and Grandmother. When Father finished
the spicy pickled cabbage, Mother brought in another
bowl. She looked a little flushed and her movements
were stiff from not wanting to make any mistakes.

After dinner, while we ate white peaches and juicy
grapes, Father told us more about his trip. Father was
always relaxed and talkative when he returned from a
trip, even though he complained of the long flights and
meals without *kimchee*.

"I like America. Everyone minds his business,"
Father said.

"What does that mean?" Grandmother asked.

"People don't concern themselves with other
people's business. They don't meddle." Father spat out
the grape seeds.

"No wonder America is full of lonely people,"
Grandmother replied.

"Were their eyes really blue?" We always asked this question because we couldn't imagine anything other than dolls having blue eyes and yellow hair.

"Not all of them, just some," he said.

"Were they really tall?" We had heard Americans were twice as tall as Koreans.

"Some, not all."

Father was getting ready to tell us something. He cleared his throat.

"I was always the first in line to order meals because no one else in our group spoke English too well. After I ordered, everyone behind me ordered 'the same.' The sergeant chef came to me on the last day and said that the Korean team was very unified, so much so that we would even order the same food every day. He didn't know it was because no one else knew how to order in English."

We all laughed, even Pyungsoo.

That night we went to sleep with our coin purses above our heads. In the middle of the night voices woke me up. First I thought it was Mother calming Pyungsoo after a nightmare; then I remembered Pyungsoo was back in Grandmother's room.

"I think I ate too much oily food. They had butter in everything."

"Do you want some digestive pills?" Mother asked quietly.

"No, I'll just see how I feel tomorrow morning."

"Maybe it isn't the butter but too much *kimchee*."

After a pause she said, "The children are on their summer recess."

"You plan the vacation and clear it with Mother."

"It seemed long this time," Mother said in a shy tone we hardly ever heard.

Father didn't answer but turned away, and soon he was snoring again.

CHAPTER 7

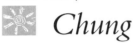 *Chung*

When I woke the next morning, Father and Grandmother were in the living area talking about Pyungsoo.

"What about an orphanage?" Father asked.

"They only get one meal a day in a place like that."

"What about Aunt's house?" Our great-aunt was very
wealthy and had many poor relations working for her.

"I don't want to add to the number of people
depending on her."

"Just don't get attached to him," Father said firmly.

At breakfast Pyungsoo bowed to say good morning,
but Father just grunted. Pyungsoo ended up sitting next
to Changhee Uhnni, who elbowed him throughout
the meal.

It was Saturday, and Father normally worked a half
day. But he said he needed to rest. Grandmother left to
go to Auntie's and took Pyungsoo with her. After

Grandmother left, Mother brought out our report cards and sat next to Father.

As she handed over the first report card she said, "Changhee did very well last semester again. Five 100's and two 98's." Mother talked most with Father about how well we did in school.

"Good," Father said, and Changhee Uhnni smiled shyly, lowering her eyes.

"She was the first in her entire class." Mother added, "Out of two hundred students."

"Very good."

Then she showed him mine.

"Still behind in math." Father frowned.

I received above 92 in every subject except in math, in which I got an 85. I was always struggling with math.

"Junehee won a writing contest in school." Mother showed him the composition with a little pink tag that said "First Place."

Father just glanced at it and said, "Good girl."

I wanted him to read it. I had written about our family: how we were often called the daughter-wealthy family, how sad I was when Father went away on his trips, and how happy I was when he returned.

"Do you remember the composition she wrote in first grade?" Mother asked, and Father shook his head. "The one with a question mark at the end of every sentence? I thought she couldn't write at all." Mother smiled.

I did bring home a page full of question marks because I had many questions. When Mother read my teacher's note, she made me rewrite it.

Moonhee, who was in the first grade, generally did better than I, but not as well as Changhee Uhnni.

"You are behind in gym again. That's what happens when you don't eat well."

Moonhee pursed her lips. Father didn't say anything about the three 100's on her report card.

"Since they did so well, how about taking the children out for dumplings?" Mother asked boldly.

All of us looked at Father eagerly.

"We'll see," Father said after staring at the floor. "I'll rest a little more, then we'll see."

"Of course," Mother said, "if you are too tired."

"We'll see, maybe." Then Father lit his cigarette and opened up the newspaper.

Mother smiled a little and smoothed her hair, sticking the loose ends into the bun.

We always tried not to get excited about Father's half promises, but we waited for them anyway. The last time we did anything with him was when he took us for a walk up the mountain in our neighborhood. Every step of the way he explained how good walking was for our body and showed us how to breathe in the clean air. He went ahead of us on the trail and we panted behind him. I held Keehee's hand and tried to follow Father as closely as possible. It was the beginning of spring and the mountain was full of forsythias, but we didn't get a chance to stop and look at them.

We wouldn't have believed that Father had once cuddled and played with us if it weren't for the few photographs in Changhee Uhnni's and my albums. She had a photograph from her hundredth-day celebration and one from her first birthday. Both times Father was holding her in front of a large table set up for the celebration. By the way he held his head stiffly, it seemed there were guests watching him.

In my photo album, Father was holding me on his lap and I was licking an apple in my hand. Mother stood behind him with her hand on his right shoulder. There were several shots of us on the same day: one with just Father and me, and another with just Mother and me. I noticed that in all the photographs Father was smiling widely, a kind of smile we rarely saw anymore. Mother said that was the year they lived without Grandmother, who had gone over to Auntie Yunekyung's to help her while Uncle was away on business.

In another photograph, I was standing next to Father at Kimpo Airport. I had on my best red dress, ruffled socks, and patent-leather shoes. Father's lips were pulled down, as they often were, in his military position. Mother said when he was walking down the runway to the plane, I kept lifting the skirt of the dress to my face and crying out. I asked Mother why I was the only one to go to the airport, and she said she didn't remember, maybe the other children were sick.

But I remembered what Auntie Yunekyung said about Father and me when no one was around. She said that I was the only one Father came to the hospital for when I was born, and the only one he spent a lot of time with when I was a baby. Auntie even admitted that Father loved me the most. She said he had the most *chung* toward me. I wasn't sure what *chung* meant exactly, even though adults talked about it all the time, especially when sad things happened. They said how could so-and-so do this when they had so much *chung* for them. Mother said that it was deeper than love. *Chung* was an attachment that grew with time and sharing. Even if you didn't like someone, you could still have much *chung* for them.

I never told this to anyone because when we asked our mother who she loved most, she said she loved us equally. Even though I wanted Mother to love me the most, I thought that was fair. Still, I was secretly glad about Father. When Changhee Uhnni accused me of having heard that I was his favorite, I even denied it.

I just said, "Why do you say that? Mother said he loved us equally." But she never believed me.

Father didn't treat me any differently. But once in a while, if something had to be brought to him, like dry socks or a cup of hot barley tea, Mother asked me to do it. I wasn't afraid of him when we were alone because sometimes I could make him smile. I said things like, "Here are your socks—if you put them on your hands they become mittens, and if you put them on your feet they become socks," or "Hot barley tea will wash the rice all the way down to your toes." First Father resisted, then his mouth stretched slowly across his face. But we were hardly ever alone, and when he was in his silent mood, I couldn't make him even look at me.

Moonhee and Keehee didn't have any baby pho-tographs. It made me feel sorry for them when Auntie

Yunekyung said that Father was so disappointed he didn't even come to the hospital when they were born.

Moonhee and I whispered in Soonja Uhnni's room, where we sometimes went to hold secret talks. It was small and dark and smelled of dampness. Even though she had been with us for three years, Soonja Uhnni never unpacked her suitcase, as if she would be returning home any day.

We were excited about getting to eat out.

"Do you think Father will let Pyungsoo Opa come with us?" Moonhee asked.

"Probably not."

"But we can't just leave him here. Can we?"

I didn't say anything.

"Do you think Father will let Pyungsoo Opa come with us on our vacation?"

"No, Moonhee."

"He will be sad if he can't come with us. Maybe we can bring home some crab legs from the sea."

We always bought crab legs from the vendors when we went on our vacation to the beach. They were one of Moonhee's favorite foods.

"That would be nice if we could do that." Moonhee smiled. "Pyungsoo Opa would like that."

I nodded, but I didn't want anything to ruin our vacation, not even Pyungsoo. It was the only time we did anything fun with Father.

·   ·   ·

Grandmother returned with Pyungsoo around lunch-time.

"Soonja," Grandmother called. "What are you making for lunch?"

Soonja Uhnni came out of the kitchen. "I don't know. Their mother didn't tell me yet."

Mother came out from the vegetable garden.

"Changhee's Mother, how about some noodle soup?" Grandmother asked.

"Yes," Mother said, but I could see that she was waiting for Father to say something. He didn't. Instead, he snapped his newspaper loudly and buried his face in it.

"We are not having dumplings?" I asked Father.

"What dumplings?" Grandmother asked.

"Father said—"

"Junehee," Mother warned me.

"You wanted dumplings?" Grandmother turned around and asked Father.

"No, noodle soup is fine," he said without looking at any of us, and went back to reading.

Changhee Uhnni glared at Father as if she were trying to burn a hole in his paper, and Moonhee and Keehee just pouted. I told myself that I knew all along he wouldn't buy us a treat.

We ate the noodle soup while Grandmother chattered on about Auntie to Father, who nodded from time to time while shoving the thin strings into his mouth. I saw how disappointed Mother was by the way she ate very quickly. She left the table as soon as Grandmother put down her chopsticks and didn't join us for peaches.

CHAPTER 8

Park Pyungsoo

"This year's peaches are delicious," Grandmother said as she peeled the thin white skin off in strips with a knife. Then she sliced each one in half to take out the pit and cut the juicy meat into quarter moons before spearing them with small fruit forks. She handed the first one to Father and he ate carefully, making sure the juice didn't drop on the wooden floor.

Pyungsoo picked up a slice but it slipped off his fruit fork, dropped on his shorts, then slid on the floor. He tried to pick it up but it kept sliding away from him toward Father. Without looking at Father, I grabbed it and put it on the tray, but I saw from the corner of my eye Father wagging his finger.

Pyungsoo wiped his hand on his shorts.

"No, don't wipe it on your shorts."

Pyungsoo wiped his hand on his shirt.

"Stop that!" Father yelled, and Pyungsoo froze.

As I got up to get a towel, Mother stepped quickly over the high threshold of the kitchen. "What happened?"

"He . . . he . . . Clean him up. It's all over his shorts and shirt."

"What is? Peach juice?" Mother asked, but Father didn't answer. "It's just some peach juice," Mother said quietly.

"What?" Father's eyes became triangles.

"It was an accident." Grandmother tried to smooth things over. "Changhee's Mother will clean him."

"I said get moving this minute!" Father shouted at Pyungsoo, then when Pyungsoo didn't move, he glared at him in astonishment.

Mother put out her hand, and Pyungsoo put on his shoes and followed Mother into the kitchen.

"Just . . . just . . . find him a home." Father talked to Mother's back, then turned to Grandmother. "What about your church? Isn't there anyone who can take him? What do ministers do if they can't find a home for an orphan?"

"I'll ask around, I said." Grandmother studied Father's irritated expression and added, "You didn't have to yell at the boy."

Father was strange that way. He became mean when he disappointed us.

I put on my shoes and went to the kitchen. Mother was wiping Pyungsoo's shorts with a wet towel.

"Junehee, can you stay with Pyungsoo?" Mother meant for me to keep him out of Father's way.

I led Pyungsoo through the back door of the kitchen to the narrow path behind the house that bent around to the small backyard. We walked under the overhanging eaves, protected from the drizzle.

Star, who was on a leash, rushed out of his doghouse barking excitedly when he saw Pyungsoo, and Pyungsoo ran away. Even though I told him there was nothing to be afraid of, we ended up squatting by the cherry tree, away from Star and under the eaves.

"My father doesn't like anything messy," I said.

Pyungsoo didn't say anything. He just sulked with his chin on his knee and poked the wet ground with a twig.

"Your father doesn't like me, your older sister doesn't like me . . ." He talked without taking his chin off his knee so his teeth clattered.

"It's not that . . ."

Pyungsoo sighed loudly, like an adult, which made his big ears move slightly up and down along with his shoulders.

"You want to make something?" I said when I couldn't think of anything to say to cheer him up.

"What?"

"I don't know, just something," I said, pulling the weeds out from the cracks between the walkway stones.

Pyungsoo took out the orange shovel from his pocket and started digging the wet earth with it.

"Watch," he said, then scooped the earth and built a small mound.

"What is it?"

"Watch." He made several more small mounds.

"What is it?" I asked again.

"My family's tombs, all four of them."

"You can't build your family's tombs here!"

"Why not?"

"It's not proper. We have to go to the mountains."

"But . . . but . . . there is no more mountain where I used to live." Pyungsoo put his chin on his knee and sulked again.

"I guess then it is all right to build the tombs here."

Pyungsoo dug some more earth and made the mounds bigger. I cut up little weeds with a sharp stone and stuck them on the mounds, and they looked like real tombs. Then I looked for something to decorate them with. I pulled the little red and pink petals of *bong-sunwha* and put them on top of the tombs. When I finished decorating the tombs, Pyungsoo got up and did the ceremonial bow. He put both of his hands up by his forehead, saluting, and slowly lowered himself onto the dry part of the ground until he was sitting down, then bent over three times, his hands touching the earth.

"Wait, we have to offer up some food," I said.

I had watched adults offer food and drinks on the Harvest Moon day in September, and on the anniversary date of our ancestors' deaths. On those days, all the relatives came to the mountain where the tombs were and set up a table full of dates, pressed meat, mung-bean pancakes, sweet rice cakes, round pears, and apples. Then they bowed, and sometimes older relatives cried and even wailed. Afterward they drank rice wine or potato liquor and ate while reminiscing.

Pyungsoo and I scrounged around for food. I went to see what was left in Star's bowl, but only a little rice was stuck on the side. When I took that, Star rushed out from his house and barked at me. I ran away and went over to the cherry tree to look for some fallen cherries on the ground. Pyungsoo found a dead cicada and some spiders. We arranged them neatly on a piece of brick that served as a table, and put it in front of the tombs.

Pyungsoo pretended to drink some rice wine from a rolled leaf. He drank half turned away, as the adults did if anyone older was present. He wrote the names of his family next to the tombs, then wrote his own name, Park Pyungsoo.

"You can't write your own name next to your family like that. You are not dead," I said.

"When I'm dead, I want my name to be right next to my father's. Don't you?" he asked.

"No, next to my mother's."

"It will be next to your husband's."

"I'm not getting married."

"Everyone gets married."

"I'm not. I'm going to live with my mother forever and ever."

"Everyone gets married," he said, not looking up from his tombs.

"I said I'm not, stupid!"

That made him be quiet.

I felt bad that I called him stupid. If Mother heard me, she would have scolded me. It rained harder. I put small pebbles around the tombs so they wouldn't wash away.

"What branch of Park are you, anyway?" I spoke first.

"Bunnam," he said, rearranging the pebbles around the tombs.

"I never heard of that Park." Grandmother told us that we could tell people's lineage by learning their ancestors' original village.

"What kind of Lee are you?" he asked.

"Chungsun Lee."

"What does your name stand for in Chinese characters?" I asked. Even though we had to wait until we went to junior high school to study Chinese characters, we learned from adults what our names meant.

"Pyung stands for 'warrior' and Soo stands for 'head.' It means a head warrior. What does Junehee stand for?"

"If I were a boy, it would be an outstanding leader, but for me, it means prominent beauty."

"A leader and a warrior," Pyungsoo said. "We can fight together." He smiled. "Isn't your father in the army?"

I nodded.

"He fights?"

I shook my head. "No, he teaches."

"What does he teach?"

"Maybe how to fight, I don't know. What does your father do? I mean . . . what did he do?"

"He was a merchant."

"Merchant? You mean he sold things? What did he sell?"

Pyungsoo said quietly, "Vegetables."

We heard someone's footsteps coming toward us. I was relieved because I didn't know what to say to Pyungsoo. Selling vegetables was a poor person's job.

Soonja Uhnni said it was time to go to the communal bath. On Saturdays, we went with our Mother to clean ourselves thoroughly.

Changhee Uhnni didn't want to go with the boy, so the four of us walked with our mother to the Dongwon bath house, which was five blocks away from our house.

I held the wash basin and walked with Pyungsoo behind Mother. Mother held Keehee's and Moonhee's hands. The rain stopped for the time being.

The Dongwon bath house was full on Saturdays. The changing room had lockers for our clothes, a big mirror, and a large scale that read in kilograms. Along the middle were narrow benches where some puffy-looking naked women drank cold drinks and combed their hair.

Steam drifted out from inside every time someone opened the door to the large room that held a huge tub. Mother helped Moonhee and Keehee undress and then undressed herself. I took off my clothes behind the locker door and put a towel around me. Pyungsoo just stood there until Mother bent down and pulled his shirt over his head and slid his shorts and underwear down. His chest was bony and his legs looked very skinny next to Mother's large thighs.

We went into the steamy room. First we washed ourselves quickly by the water faucets, then we stood by the hot tub, waiting for Mother to go in. She slowly dunked her body and sighed contentedly. The water was always too hot for us and it took us longer to immerse ourselves, but when we did, we felt a kind of chill we liked. Pyungsoo stood in the water up to his thighs, wincing, and Mother came over, put her arms around him, and sank slowly. She sat there with him until his shoulders relaxed.

After a while, everyone's face turned red and we were glad to get out of the tub. I sat with my knees pulled up and watched Moonhee and Keehee playing with the water in the basin. Pyungsoo was on the other side of Mother. When Mother finished washing herself, she started with me. She rubbed me with a small red towel until all the dead skin came off, then poured water over me. Next she cleaned Moonhee and Keehee, then Pyungsoo was last. She rubbed gingerly around his knee scabs and cleaned the rest of his body briskly. When she poured hot water on him, he shrank back, then shook himself like Star.

By the time we were finished, we were glad to get out to the cool changing room. I dried quickly, put on my clothes, and helped Keehee get dressed while Mother dried Pyungsoo. She toweled his back, under his arms, and between his legs.

CHAPTER 9

 Friends and Father

On Sunday morning we put on our best clothes to get ready for church. A white poplin shirt with a checkered skirt for Changhee Uhnni, a white blouse and a gray pleated skirt with pink polka dots for me, a sky blue dress for Moonhee, and a navy dress with white piping for Keehee. Pyungsoo wore what he always wore, gray shorts and a striped shirt.

As Mother brushed her hair to put it into a bun, she said to Father, "It's been a long time—how about going to church with us?"

Father shook his head and drew on his cigarette.

"What about after church? Maybe we could have dumplings or noodles. Mother will be late coming back," our mother said in her trying-to-be-cheerful voice. "We didn't get to go out yesterday. You said . . ."

"I didn't promise anything."

"No, you didn't. What about today?"

Father shook his head.

"You never spend—"

"What?" Father's eyes sharpened.

"The children need to spend a little time with their father," Mother appealed.

"Why don't you let your good priest-friend take them out?" Father said coldly.

"Good priest-friend?" Mother spoke slowly.

"Father Cho, the one that you respect so much. He took them out on Children's Day, I hear. Why don't you ask him?"

"Respect?" Mother started, then she sighed. "You don't understand anything."

"No, I don't. I'm not as holy as your brother or your friend." Father drew on his cigarette. "Anyway, I may go out later."

"Where?"

"Just out."

Mother sighed again and brushed her hair so hard that we could hear the bristles going through it. Then she put down the brush with a clank.

The six of us, including Pyungsoo, left for church. Mother was agitated at first. She didn't want any of us to hold her hands. Then, by the way her eyelids started to droop, I knew she was more sad than angry. I just hoped Father Cho had his funny stories today.

Father Cho, our pastor, was Mother's childhood friend and the best friend of her priest-brother. Whenever he wasn't busy he spent some time with us. After the Mass, Father Cho stood at the end of the staircase and greeted the parishioners. He signaled us to wait.

"Who's the boy?" he asked as we followed him to his office.

"He is our guest," Mother answered.

"I bet you get all the attention in that family," Father Cho said playfully.

If it wasn't Father Cho, Mother would have tilted her head back a little, putting on her proud face.

"Cola? Juice?" Father Cho asked, and brought out the refreshments. We sat on his old couch with our feet dangling.

"Changhee was first in her class last quarter." Mother smiled at Changhee Uhnni.

"Oh? I am very impressed. We have to celebrate." Father Cho stuck out his hand, and Changhee Uhnni smiled widely and shook it.

"The second student was seven points behind me," she boasted.

"Is that so?" Father Cho said. "What do you want, dumplings? *Bulgoki?*"

"*Bulgoki!*" she said. Marinated beef was her favorite.

"Another day," Mother interrupted. "Their father came home yesterday from a trip."

We were disappointed, but Father Cho started to tell us a story and soon we forgot about it. He said he had just attended a wedding and the bridegroom was very handsome and the bride very pretty. Except for one thing, they were a match made in heaven. We asked what that was, and he said the wife was twice as tall as the husband. We all laughed and Mother accused Father

Cho of making up the story. No man would marry a woman that tall, however pretty, Mother said. Then Father Cho smiled and went on to other stories. I watched Mother's droopy eyes lift.

Whenever Mother was with her friends and family, she laughed and said many clever things. Whether it was our priest-uncle's birthday or a celebration for our maternal grandmother, Mother was always the center of attention.

Many of our priest-uncle's friends were also Mother's childhood friends, and they liked talking about her to us. On our uncle's last birthday, one friend said to us, "Did you know that your mother was the best athlete when she was young?" When we shook our heads he said, "She outran all of us."

"I can still outrun you all," Mother challenged him.

He put up his hands and said, "No doubt. We wouldn't want to try. We don't want to look foolish in front of the children." And they all laughed.

Another friend said Mother made him climb a persimmon tree to pick fruit, and when the owner came by, she ran away and left him there to take the blame.

Mother often had the last word, which made them say to us, "Your mother, she wears the pants in your house, doesn't she?"

We nodded even though we didn't know exactly what that meant.

But with Father and his relatives Mother was just polite, and at home we hardly ever saw Mother laughing and making jokes with Father. On those rare occasions when Father did join us at our maternal grandmother's house, he just sat there and nodded at Mother's comments. Mother wasn't as clever with her friends when Father was around.

We returned home from church and Father had gone out. Soonja Uhnni said he would be out late. Mother just sighed and told us to change out of our clothes.

"We should have gone out with Father Cho," Changhee Uhnni said angrily when I closed the door. "He was going to buy me *bulgoki*. Why did we have to come home? He's not even here. He's never here."

When we came out of our room, Mother was making omelet rice—fried rice with vegetables and a layer of egg on top. We loved this dish and it was almost as good as eating out. Mother said that she might be able to take us out for dumplings or *bulgoki* soon since we all did well in school. That made all of us feel better, especially Changhee Uhnni.

Grandmother hadn't returned by the time we finished lunch, and we lay in the living area and let Mother fan us. Pyungsoo lay next to me, farthest away from Changhee Uhnni, and every time Mother's fan came above his head, he closed his eyes. Mother hummed a lullaby but she sounded sad.

I got up and went to the big room and brought out Mother's photo album. Sometimes Mother cheered up when she looked at old photographs and told us stories. I opened to the first page and put the album down on her legs. Changhee Uhnni flipped over to her stomach, and Moonhee and Keehee sat up next to Mother. Pyungsoo and I knelt behind Moonhee.

"You want to look at the photographs?" Mother asked.

I nodded.

She turned the pages slowly until she came to the photographs of her in junior high and high school, on class trips and graduations. Her hair was cut just below her ears, and it was parted on the right side. All her classmates had the same hairstyle and they wore uniforms, dark jackets with white round collars and pleated skirts that came below the knees.

"How old were you here, Mother?" Moonhee pointed.

"Fifteen. I was the only privileged one from my neighborhood who was sent to Seoul to go to a boarding school." Mother touched the photographs. "I haven't seen these friends in a long time. We were so close. Everything changes when you get married."

She turned some more pages, and I stopped her where our favorite photograph was. It was a small picture of our parents walking down the street before their engagement. Father was in his uniform and Mother in a flowery *hanbok*, a traditional costume of a short jacket with half-moon–shaped sleeves and long flowing ribbons, and a floor-length skirt that spread out like a tent. It seemed like a warm day and her thin *hanbok* was flowing in the wind. Mother's hair was down, not in a bun as we knew her, and her face was rounder. She and Father were both smiling at the photographer. The thing we noticed every time was that Father was carrying Mother's handbag. We hadn't ever seen our father do that.

"Why was Father carrying your bag?" I asked, even though I knew the answer.

"He thought it was too heavy for me." Mother sighed and looked at the photograph longingly.

I turned some more pages until I came to the biggest wedding photograph. On the bottom was printed in white letters, 1953, DECEMBER 3.

"Myungdong Church?" Moonhee asked, and Mother nodded. It was a Catholic church in Seoul.

"Your grandmother didn't like that." Mother said that every time we looked at this photograph.

I once overheard Auntie Yunekyung say Grandmother didn't want Father to marry Mother because she was Catholic, unlike Grandmother, who was a Methodist, and because Mother was a year older than Father. But Father didn't give up. He said to Grandmother, "You'll see, you won't ever regret it. She is a good person. She is far better than I will ever be, and she will be a good daughter-in-law for you." That was the first time Father disobeyed his mother. The only things Grandmother liked about Mother were that they were from the same northern city, Pyongyang, and that at least she was a Christian in a Buddhist country.

In the big wedding photograph, Father wore his military uniform, a special one with the medals on his left chest, and Mother wore a white wedding *hanbok* and veil. Mother's face was lowered, as if she were looking at the chrysanthemums held in her hands. On both Mother's and Father's heads and shoulders were squiggly confetti and dots of rice.

"I was so nervous. My hands shook the whole time," Mother said.

In the background were Grandmother, Great-Aunt,

and Father's cousins and friends, some we knew and some we had never seen. From Mother's side was her priest-brother, our maternal grandmother, Mother's best friend, Mrs. Park, and her cousins and friends. They all looked either cold or angry.

There were no honeymoon photographs. Mother said it was a difficult time after the war. But she always added that even then, the first year they lived by themselves in a rented room was like a honeymoon.

Usually after looking at the photographs, I asked her to tell us about how she met Father. Then Mother smiled a little, stretched her legs, and told us the story. But today she just closed the photo album and looked away toward the rose garden. We lay down again and she fanned us, humming a tune.

I closed my eyes and tried to remember the story.

During the war Mother's uncle, who was a general in the army, found her a job. Mother became a secretary at the translation department, where they took new types of weapons or new war tactics from America and gave them Korean names. Father was in charge of the translations.

Mother said when Father wanted her to do something, he was courteous and exact, not like the other officers, who came in and blurted out the things they wanted. Father also had the best posture and the neatest uniform.

Soon Mother heard the secretaries from different departments talking about Officer Lee. They thought he was the handsomest man around and envied Mother for working for him. Even though Mother thought Father was attractive, she was suspicious of any man who had women talking about him constantly. She paid little attention to Father and was very formal with him.

Other secretaries treated her coolly and didn't invite her to have lunch with them. First she didn't think much of it. Then she thought maybe they were jealous because she was related to a high-ranking officer. Finally one of them said, "So you and Officer Lee are dating?"

Mother was very angry that Father had spread a false rumor. From that day on, she ignored him as much as she could. When Father asked her if anything was wrong, Mother told him about the rumor. Father said he had not spread the rumor but perhaps his feelings about her showed. He said all this standing straight, with his hands on his back, as if he were reporting an incident. Mother was impressed. She thought anyone who was that honest deserved a chance.

Only after she had married him did she find out that he came from a very reputable family who owned a lot of land. Father said, "It doesn't matter who I am related to. I am exactly as I show you, nothing more and nothing less." But Mother knew many men who would boast about an important relative, even if he was their twice-removed cousin's friend.

It wasn't hard to see Father having a clean uniform or a very straight posture, or being honest about his family. But it was difficult to imagine Father holding Mother's hand, which she admitted they did in movie theaters. Mother's hands were large and soft and moved quickly and easily to make hot soup or rub our stomachs. Father's hands were even and his fingernails were always perfect, not too long or short. Mother said she liked his hands because they seemed like hands that would not hurry or change.

There were hardly any photographs of Mother and Father together after we were born. Mother said that's how things were after marriage. In the few photographs from important days such as Great-Aunt's sixtieth birthday, Father's cousin's wedding, and Grandmother's birthday, often Father and Mother didn't even stand next to one another. The most recent photograph was from our vacation two years ago at the military officers' resort. A sergeant took a picture of Father and Mother in bathing suits squinting into the sun.

When Grandmother looked at the photographs from our vacation, she commented on our bathing suits. "You mean you sat around the beach naked like this?"

We said, "We weren't naked. We were wearing bathing suits." But she still thought it was like being naked.

"I can't even wear what I want when I'm away from this place," Mother muttered to herself.

CHAPTER 10

 Our Room

Two days after the peach incident, Mother and Soonja Uhnni cleaned the vacant room that had been closed to save expenses. The room was in the right wing, in one of the two corners farthest from the main part of the house, and on the same side as the storage room, the bathroom, and the entrance area. Grandmother said we were to share this room with Pyungsoo when Father was home, but it belonged to Changhee Uhnni and me. She thought we were finally old enough to have a room of our own. I was excited, even if it meant sharing it with Changhee Uhnni, and I hoped that she would be nicer to Pyungsoo since it was because of him the room had been opened up for us.

Soonja Uhnni took out the old blankets stored in there for winter and brought in summer blankets and bedding for us. She cleaned out the drawers of the clothing cabinet and filled them with our summer clothes, then carried out the old chest and a broken table to the storage room. Mother wiped the walls with a wet rag to make sure there was no mold or spider-webs, and mended some holes in the rice paper on the sliding wooden-framed doors. Afterward Mother had Soonja Uhnni put hot coals in the cavern underneath the *ondol*, the stone floor, to dry the damp room.

Mother set a study table in the middle of the floor and put down some straw seat cushions for us. Chang-hee Uhnni and I brought in our schoolbooks and the Fifty Best Children's Books series and arranged them on a bookcase that was already in the room. When all was finished, Mother left the room, instructing Changhee Uhnni to act like a big sister and to share the room with us and Pyungsoo generously. But as soon as Mother left, Changhee Uhnni walked around the room and sur-veyed it, then took a black crayon out of the box and drew a cross on the floor, dividing the room into four sections. She dragged the table to her corner.

"This is my square." She pointed to the floor where she stood. "That's yours." She gave me the square diago-nally across from her and gave the two remaining squares to Moonhee and Keehee.

Pyungsoo stood where he was, in Moonhee's square.

"Where is Pyungsoo's?" I asked, knowing there wasn't one.

Changhee Uhnni turned away and opened her sketch-book, ignoring me.

"He can stay in mine," offered Moonhee, who hated conflict.

"Don't give him any space unless you want your square taken away," Changhee Uhnni said sharply.

"Mother said for us to share the room," I said.

"So?"

"So, where is Pyungsoo's square?"

"I'm in charge—I can do whatever I please," she said. Pyungsoo inched toward me. "No, you can't stay there either," she shouted, and he froze.

"You can stay in mine," I said to Pyungsoo.

"No, he can't."

"Why not? I can do whatever I want with my square. Besides, this room is half mine."

"I am in charge. Only one person to a square." Changhee Uhnni was using Father's military voice, loud with evenly spaced words.

I took out a crayon and drew a line down my square.

"Two squares, one for me and one for Pyungsoo."

Changhee Uhnni scowled at me, muttering something like "We'll see" under her breath, but didn't order me anymore.

No one said anything for a while. Moonhee handed us each a piece of paper, and we began to draw. That was what Mother did sometimes when we didn't get along. She made us be quiet and draw. I didn't have to see to know that Changhee Uhnni was drawing sharp, angular lines. I could hear the harsh scratching sound of crayon on the paper. Moonhee was drawing thin lines to make flowers, and Keehee drew bold round lines with a red crayon. She loved to draw the sun. I drew all of us jumping rope in the yard on a sunny day. Pyungsoo helped me by coloring the background in sky blue.

Grandmother slid open the wooden door and winced. "*Ahigo*, who drew on the floor?"

We did not answer. Changhee Uhnni finally turned

around and said, "I did, Grandmother, because of the boy. I didn't want him to come into my space."

"Your space? Do you own this room? Can't you get along with anyone?" she sighed.

"I get along with whoever I want."

"Who is that?"

"People I like."

"Who do you like?" Grandmother asked in her sarcastic tone, then softened a little. "If you get along with the boy, I'll take you with me the next time I go to your great-aunt's."

Grandmother's older sister lived in a house so big that we could not count all the rooms, and there were peacocks on her large, beautiful grounds.

"I don't want to go there," Changhee Uhnni said.

"You always want to go there."

"I don't want to."

Grandmother shook her head. "You are just as stubborn as your father."

"I'm not like Father!" Changhee Uhnni yelled back.

"You are just like him."

"Then Grandmother is stubborn too. You are his mother."

"I apologize," Mother said, approaching from behind. "It's my fault that my child knows how to talk back. Apologize to Grandmother."

"Why does everyone say I'm like Father?" Changhee Uhnni asked, no longer mean but hurt.

"Apologize," Mother said in her deep voice.

"I was wrong. I'm sorry," she said without looking at Grandmother.

"If you get along with Pyungsoo, I'll buy you something you want," Grandmother coaxed her one more time, and walked away.

"What did I ask you to do?" Mother asked.

"I'm sorry. I'll erase the crayon."

"Don't disappoint me anymore," Mother said in her angry tone, and closed the door tightly.

Changhee Uhnni wiped off the crayon with a tissue, muttering, "She's stubborn, I'm not stubborn. . . . She . . ."

Changhee Uhnni was right, even though she shouldn't have talked back to Grandmother. Grandmother didn't listen to anyone. If Mother said we had enough rice, Grandmother would nod but make her buy more anyway, and if I said I washed my hands, she would insist that I wash them again. Maybe she seemed stubborn because she didn't believe anyone.

Father was stubborn in a different way. When he made up his mind about something, he never changed it. If he said he didn't want to go to so-and-so's house for a birthday celebration, it didn't matter what Mother said or how she pleaded, he didn't go. It was best not to ask him in a way that forced him to choose yes or no, but in a way to give him room to think he could change his mind.

Changhee Uhnni was more like Father in that way. She didn't change her mind easily about anything. Even when she erased the crayon, she said, "Remember your square." The rest of us shared our space and made sure we didn't step on hers. Even when we had to go to the bathroom, we used one of the sliding double doors that was on Moonhee's side. Pyungsoo was especially careful.

That night Changhee Uhnni divided the room in

half and told me to sleep on my side. In the middle of the night she kicked my feet and woke me up because my foot crossed the line. She lost sleep so she could guard her space. Even though Changhee Uhnni was often mean, I felt sorry for her sometimes because she couldn't help the way she was, and because she got blamed first for everything, especially by Father.

CHAPTER 11

 Grandmother

Grandmother announced next morning that she was
going to visit the Kims. She said it had been over a week
since the boy came to our home, and now that the rain
had stopped, she was going to start visiting her church
friends to see if anyone could take Pyungsoo in. She
thought the Kims, who were middle-aged and could
not have any children, might be her best bet.

Father stopped eating and said, "If anyone—anyone—
wants to take the boy for any reason, hand him over to
them immediately."

Mother kept her eyes on the boy, who sat there with
his head lowered and his big ears turning red.

After the breakfast dishes were cleared, Grandmother
began preparing for the outing. She sat in front of her
dresser and put on a dab of face cream, then rubbed on
some foundation before patting on Coty face powder.
She carefully drew in her eyebrows and put on crimson-

colored lipstick, spreading it evenly with her fourth finger. She combed her hair back and put it in a bun, then she attached a fake bun to make her hair look fuller and checked it with a round hand mirror.

Mother said Grandmother was very pretty when she was young, but we couldn't see how that could have been. She had small eyes with thin eyelids, a long, narrow nose that flared out a little too much, and skinny lips. To us, she looked small and wrinkled with or without her makeup, and smaller and more wrinkled without her clothes. When Grandmother took out her dentures at night, her mouth caved in and she looked very ugly.

Grandmother said it was a curse that she had been so pretty. If she had been more plain, her husband would not have married her, and then she would not have been abandoned at the age of twenty-one.

Grandmother opened the brown lacquer cabinet and took out her pale blue *hanbok* and tried it on. Then she changed to a pale yellow one, and then to a bright green one. She went through this routine of changing her clothes every time she went out. Nothing satisfied Grandmother easily. She kept asking herself, "Is this proper enough, is that proper enough?" It didn't seem she owned anything that was proper enough for any occasion.

When she finally selected the bright yellow skirt and the coral-colored jacket with no ribbons, she went through her brooch box and tried every one of her brooches against her jacket before ending up wearing the tear-shaped opal one. Next she went through her ring box. That was easier. She wore a diamond ring set in a delicately designed white gold band on the third finger of her right hand, and two jade bands on the fourth finger of her left hand.

She put on a pair of *bosun*, socks shaped like boots. Then she was ready. After looking at herself in the mirror one more time, she took her white beaded handbag, went outside, and slipped her small feet into her *komooshin*.

"Changhee's Mother, I'm leaving," she said, and Mother and Soonja Uhnni came out of the kitchen and bowed. "Don't forget to cut some roses and bring them in, and wash my handkerchiefs."

Both Mother and Soonja Uhnni answered, "Yes."

After Grandmother left for the Kims, Mother came into the living area and stretched her legs and massaged her forearm.

"Can we have some popped corn or rice?" I asked. Sometimes when Grandmother wasn't home, Mother had Soonja Uhnni bring a bowl of corn or rice and had the man under the railroad bridge pop it for a hundred won.

Mother sent Soonja Uhnni out with a bowl of rice.

"Why does she have to change her *hanbok* so many times?" Moonhee asked. "I'm not like that, am I?"

Mother shook her head. Moonhee didn't like it when adult relatives said she took after Grandmother. I had to assure her often that I didn't see any resemblance.

"Well, that's how Grandmother is," Mother said, and sighed.

Grandmother was at her worst when she had to go to an important family gathering. On the hundredth-day celebration of her grandbaby nephew, she changed her *hanbok* five times. Then she thought it would be better if she didn't go at all since she didn't attend the other nephew's celebration. It wouldn't be proper.

Sometimes we didn't even tell Grandmother where we were going, even if it was just to a friend's, because by the time she asked all her questions, we didn't want to go anymore. When Mother wanted to go to her high school reunion, Grandmother asked what restaurant they were going to, what clothes Mother was wearing, who would come that Grandmother knew, and when Mother finally said it wasn't important that she go, Grandmother insisted that she should.

From time to time Grandmother even made us sort through our schoolbags and dresser drawers in front of her so she would know what we had, then she told us what to keep and what to use more sparingly. She didn't let us throw out anything easily. We didn't like it when we found our drawers had been rearranged while we weren't home.

Mother liked it less than we did. Once in a while when Mother wasn't home, Grandmother opened her clothing cabinet and took out all her *hanbok*, dresses, sweaters, slips—even her underclothes—and unfolded them, shaking each piece as if she expected something to fall out. Then she refolded them one by one in her own way. As she did this she commented, "This is too bright," or too big, too heavy, too dark.

When Mother saw the rearranged drawers, she would sigh deeply and say, "I don't have anything she doesn't know about. Why does she go through my things?" Carefully and quietly she refolded and rearranged each piece, but I could hear her anger by the way she shut the drawers louder than usual.

Still, Mother didn't let us complain to her about Grandmother. She said if it wasn't for Grandmother's inheritance and her careful management, we wouldn't be able to go to a private school. She said if Grandmother was particular it was because she was smart and because it was part of her personality. She reminded us to be grateful. But we couldn't be grateful toward someone who meddled in everyone's business.

Soonja Uhnni returned with the popped rice, and she sat and ate with us in the living area.

"It's so quiet here when she isn't around," Soonja Uhnni said in her heavy accent.

"Soonja," Mother chided her, and Soonja Uhnni just smiled and put some more popped rice in her mouth.

When we finished eating, Mother cleaned the floor to make sure there wasn't any popped rice on it. If Grandmother found one grain, she would ask us about it and say that it was a waste of money.

Grandmother returned from the Kims. She shook her *hanbok* skirt and washed her hands as she did after every outing. From our room I could see her looking over the yard. "Soonja!" she called, and our helper ran out. "Be careful, you broke a rose stem."

"Yes," Soonja Uhnni answered while twisting her lips to one side.

"Don't let the soapdish fill up with water."

"Yes."

"Changhee's Mother," she called. Mother came out from the kitchen. "Changhee's Mother, I think it's time for our soybean soup day, now that the rain has stopped."

"Yes, Mother, I'll start the preparation." Then Mother asked carefully, "What did the Kims say?"

"They are going to think about it, but they want to see Pyungsoo first. I invited Mrs. Kim to have some soybean soup. She doesn't know if she can come, but we should be prepared."

"Yes, I see," Mother said, and went back to the kitchen.

CHAPTER 12

 The Soybean Soup Day

Grandmother wrote down how many *mal* of soybeans we needed, changing the amount four times before she was satisfied, then told Mother to make new *kimchee* for the occasion. On the day of the soup Grandmother kept checking back in the kitchen to see that everything was in order, calling Soonja Uhnni to do this and that at the same time. Soonja Uhnni answered yes to everything but complained to Mother when Grandmother wasn't around. Mother just said, "I know. Why don't you clean the rooms first. I'll cut the *kimchee*."

Grandmother Boksoon, who was called in to help, sat in the pantry/dining room and ground the cooked soybeans on a round stone grinder. Pyungsoo sat next to his grandmother and poured the beans into the grinder whenever she nodded, and the ground beans came out from the side where two stones met. Then Mother put the ground beans into a gauze sack and squeezed out the juice, which was used for the soup.

Mother let us help her by making marble-sized balls from glutinous rice powder. We rolled the dough between our hands, trying to make perfectly round balls, but only Changhee Uhnni came close. Mother complimented her, saying she would make a good wife some day, and Changhee Uhnni smiled. Moonhee wasn't too bad at making them, but I got bored quickly and started to make squares and triangles, which Mother put in our soup later.

In the morning we ordered fresh noodles from the noodle shop. As the guests came, Soonja Uhnni dropped the noodles into the boiling water and scooped them out to be washed in cold water. The rice balls were boiled separately, then both were put into the cold soybean soup. We added big chunks of ice to the thick broth to make sure it was cold enough.

We got hungry from working all morning and ate lots of soup in the pantry/dining room. On a hot day in August, the cold noodle soup tasted good with the summer *kimchee*. Grandmother Boksoon smiled and watched Pyungsoo eat. She said again and again how his new clothes looked very nice and thanked Mother for the fourth time. Pyungsoo had on a new blue shirt-and-pants set Grandmother bought him.

Guests started to arrive around lunchtime. Grandmother's church friends and acquaintances were first; Mother's friends, including Father Cho and Mrs. Park, next; then some neighbors. The soybean soup day wasn't a formal gathering or a celebration where important friends or relatives came bearing gifts of meat or money.

Anyone could stop by and eat at our house. As usual Auntie Yunekyung came after most of the work was done and sat in the living area with the guests and ate with them.

Grandmother kept looking toward the door even when she was greeting the guests, as if she expected someone special. She grabbed each guest by their hands and said, "It's been a long time. How have you been?"

As each guest arrived, Mother came out of the kitchen with us and we all bowed. "Is this the oldest? How big she has grown." "Is this the second? She looks just like her mother." "How pretty the third one is. They do say the third daughter is the prettiest." "Youngest? Oh my, she has grown. She looks like her mother and father." They all said the same things, and Mother just smiled and said, "Yes, yes." Then they were led to the living area, where several tables had been set up.

Most of the guests brought fruit—watermelon, peaches, grapes, and plums—and some a cake or candies. Mother accepted the gifts, straightened the shoes the guests had taken off, and went back to the kitchen.

Grandmother walked around the living area and made sure everyone had seconds, even though some people said they were full. "What are you saying?" she insisted. "That was nothing," and she poured more noodles or soup into their bowls. Grandmother didn't let anyone leave the table until she thought they had enough. She even fed the postman who came to deliver the mail. When he said he didn't eat this northern food, she made him eat it anyway. Then Grandmother sent Soonja Uhnni to ask more neighbors to stop by and to invite Mrs. Kim again, but Soonja Uhnni returned and said Mrs. Kim wasn't able to come. Grandmother sent her the thickest soup.

Mother's best friend, Mrs. Park, came and sat in the pantry/dining room, where she could talk to Mother, but Grandmother insisted that was no place for a guest and made her eat in the living area. When Mother brought in more fresh noodles, Mrs. Park whispered to her, and Mother whisked the bowl away before Grandmother could see it. Father Cho sat with the ministers from Grandmother's church and politely chatted with them while fishing the noodles out of his soup. But as soon as the noodles were gone, Grandmother put in some more and wouldn't hear of him not having them. Father Cho nodded and thanked her, and then ate more slowly. This was Grandmother's way of being generous. She insisted that everyone accept what she offered.

Our maternal grandmother, Grandma Min, stopped by with our priest-uncle, and Grandmother made the most fuss about them. "How long has it been? Why don't you come visit us more often? You've gotten old." Grandmother held Grandma Min's hand and didn't let go, which made her blush. Mother came out, and they just looked at each other and nodded. Our priest-uncle gave us hugs and some candy.

When Grandma Min and Uncle sat to eat, Auntie Yunekyung got up and served them, and then began clearing dishes as if she had been working all morning. Mother sent me inside to sit with Grandma Min and Uncle, who asked me questions about school. I tried to talk to them while they ate, but Grandmother kept pouring more soup and noodles, and I ran out of things to say to them.

Then the conversation at the table turned to religion. The ministers from Grandmother's church argued with Grandma Min about the Virgin Mary. Mother came with more noodles and poked her mother's leg under the table. Still, Grandma Min didn't stop insisting on her points, which made the ministers nod and eat quickly.

Neighbors who lived in the poorer section sat by themselves around one table. They whispered loudly about the hairstylist who ran away with the coal man, and the mad dog that bit someone's maid. When Grandmother hovered around their table to pour some soup, they talked about how the room was large and the soup savory. Some accepted the soup to take home for their husbands or children.

By the time everyone left, we had served at least sixty bowls of soup, and we still had a whole basinful. Finally Father came home and ate the noodles with Grandmother, who hadn't eaten anything all day long. Auntie Yunekyung sat with them and chatted, commenting on this guest and that. Mother and Soonja Uhnni, too tired to wash any more dishes or boil any more noodles, sat and rested. Grandmother Boksoon insisted on washing the dishes, and with Pyungsoo by her side, she cleaned up the kitchen. As long as Father was there, no one mentioned that the Kims did not come.

CHAPTER 13

 The Accident

Finally the earth dried. As long as we were cooped up together, Changhee Uhnni was continuously mean to Pyungsoo, and we were glad to get away from her. Even during the summer recess, we liked going to the school grounds because there were monkey bars, a chin-up bar, a jungle gym, and a swing. Moonhee, Pyungsoo, and I walked over to the swing, which was free.

The wooden seats were damp from the humidity, but Moonhee sat on one anyway and asked me to push. "Not too hard, Uhnni." I pushed her gently and she started pumping higher. Pyungsoo got on the next swing and stood on the seat. First he seemed afraid to move, then he bent his knees and pumped his body into the air. I waited for my turn.

From a distance a boy walked in our direction, and I knew right away it was our cousin Sungjin. I could see from the way he moved forward like a bird pecking that he was crammed full of energy from having stayed inside too long. As soon as Sungjin recognized us, he ran over.

"Get off! This isn't your school," Sungjin yelled at Pyungsoo.

"Leave him alone. It's not your swing." I tried to be firm.

"Sungjin Opa," Moonhee said, "you can use mine." But he ignored her.

"Hey, go to your own stupid school. Get off!" Sungjin yelled louder.

"Sungjin, leave him alone!" I ordered.

When Pyungsoo almost came to a stop, Sungjin stood behind him and pushed Pyungsoo's back. His right foot slipped off and he tried to get his footing back, but Sungjin pushed him harder. Pyungsoo's body lurched forward and both feet were in the air. He hung on to the ropes.

"Stop it. Leave him alone!" I grabbed Sungjin's hands but he shook me off.

Pyungsoo found his footing, so our mean cousin pulled back the seat as far as he could and pushed it hard, again and again until Pyungsoo's swing was high in the air. Pyungsoo looked terrified and started to whimper.

"Stop that, stop that!" I yelled.

"Pyungsoo is a sissy, Pyungsoo is a sissy," our cousin teased while continuing to push.

Pyungsoo tried to lower himself on the seat while the swing was up in the air. One of his hands slipped off the rope and he hung on to one side with both hands. As the swing twisted back and forth, hitting the frame, he lost his footing altogether. For a brief moment his body hung diagonally in the air, then tumbled forward. With a soft thump he landed on his side, facing away from the swing.

I rushed over to him.

One side of his face was covered with mud, and blood dripped from his nose. He clenched his arm and curled up like a worm killed with salt.

"Ah—ah—ah," he moaned.

I tried to help him up but he moaned louder.

"Get up," Sungjin commanded. "Get up you sissy, there's nothing wrong with you."

He jabbed Pyungsoo with his foot, but Pyungsoo just lay there groaning.

Now Sungjin looked scared. He got down on his knees and looked at the boy's face closely.

"Can't you see he's hurt? He probably broke a bone," I yelled at him. "Run home! Get Mother!"

Sungjin got up and ran toward the gate.

Moonhee, who had been frozen on the seat of the swing, came and squatted next to me, and stroked his head like Mother did when we were sick.

Other children on the grounds quickly gathered around us.

"He's bleeding." "Take him to the hospital." "Go get the gate watcher." "Clamp your fingers around his nose."

They stood around making suggestions until Mother and Grandmother arrived without Sungjin. Mother was still wearing an apron, and even Grandmother came in her house clothes. They were out of breath, especially Grandmother.

"Ahigo." Grandmother squatted next to him, folding up her skirt so it didn't touch the ground. Mother just sat next to him and started to wipe off Pyungsoo's face with her apron, but he jerked away. Then she tried to turn him over, but Pyungsoo screamed. Finally, Mother lowered her arms and gently scooped him up, and we headed toward Dr. Pae's office. Other children followed us.

When Father saw Pyungsoo's arm in the cast he shook his head and said, *"Nachom, nachom."* This was an expression he used when he couldn't think of any words to explain the ridiculous situation at hand. Mother was feeding Pyungsoo. Not only that, but we had to eat in Grandmother's room instead of the living area because Grandmother thought Pyungsoo should be warm.

Pyungsoo had a thick white cast on his right arm and a bandage on the right side of his face where he was scraped badly. He looked worse than when he first came.

"How long does he have to be like that?" Father asked.

"Dr. Pae said maybe four weeks," Grandmother answered, "if lucky, three."

"Nachom, nachom. What did the Kims say about taking him?"

"They wanted to see him first, but we can't show him like that."

"We are going to wait until the cast comes off?" Father asked in disbelief.

"They weren't even sure they wanted a child. We can't show a child with a broken arm."

"*Nachom,*" Father said again, and scraped the ceramic rice bowl hard with his silver spoon.

Keehee finished her rice and stuck out her bowl for more. Usually she waited until Mother noticed the empty bowl. Then, when Father wasn't watching, Mother would give her some. But Mother was occupied with Pyungsoo.

Grandmother reached out to get her bowl when Father yelled, "I told you not to give her any extra food. She is too fat."

Grandmother stared at him, then said, "She is six years old."

"That's when you have to be careful."

Grandmother sighed and said, "Little children are chubby. They grow out of it."

"Don't give her any more rice!"

With her hand stretched out in the air Keehee just sat there.

"Listen to me." Father was gritting his teeth. "No one listens to me. Keehee should cut down on food and Moonhee should eat more. Can't you get that straight?"

When Keehee sighed like Mother, Father yelled, "Go to the other room."

Keehee got up slowly and walked out without having finished the soup she had been saving to eat with more rice.

Father went back to eating his food but the rest of us just sat there. Mother had stopped feeding Pyungsoo, and Moonhee started to cry. She always cried first when something bad happened.

"Stop it!" Father yelled at her. "You are too weak."

Grandmother stared at Father while he continued to eat. Her face turned as white as rice paper.

"Let me ask you this in front of your children, even if you are their father. Why are you acting like this?" Grandmother never talked to him like this with us around. Father didn't say anything. "You are going to show disrespect to me, an old woman and your only mother, by not answering me in front of your children?"

We looked to Mother to see if we should get up and leave, but her head was lowered.

"Why don't you ever listen to me?" Father put down his chopsticks and looked Grandmother directly in the eye.

"What did you say that was so important?"

"Don't feed her so much. How many times do I have to tell you?"

"She is a child. She needs to eat and grow."

"Then feed her, feed them all. Just don't tell me to be responsible."

"Yelling at a six-year-old child is your responsibility?"

"I don't want any more responsibility."

"What responsibility?" Grandmother was pointing her chopsticks at Father. She pointed when she was very angry. "What do you do? You leave the house after eating breakfast and don't come home until all your children are sleeping. Your wife raises the children and I run the house."

Grandmother's thin lips quivered.

"What responsibility? Do you come home anymore with a piece of bean cake or fruit for me and say 'Mother, I brought these for you'?" She shook her head.

"What happened to you? Why don't you come home anymore?"

Father was silent for a long time, then he said very slowly, "I can't live like this. I can't . . . I just can't . . ." His voice was strained and he spoke slower and slower. "I can't be . . . I can't live up to anybody's expectations anymore. I'm not a good son or father. You understand? Do you understand, Mother?" His voice cracked. "Do you?" Father tried to close his mouth tightly, but his mouth opened wide and he began to cry like a little boy.

Mother motioned for us to leave the room. The three of us and Pyungsoo left quietly and sat in the big room. Moonhee couldn't stop crying, so I put my arm around her shoulders. Changhee Uhnni glared at Pyungsoo with her meanest eyes. Only Keehee seemed calm, drawing in her notebook in the corner. She was drawing a black circle. Keehee rarely cried.

We heard the front door open and Auntie Yunekyung calling out, "I'm here. Where is everyone?"

Mother came out of the room and greeted her politely, and went to the kitchen. We went out and greeted Auntie, except Moonhee.

"What's the matter?" she asked.

"Nothing," I answered.

"How's the boy? That Sungjin, he's really . . . I don't know who he takes after. I told him that for the rest of the summer he can't go to the school grounds." Auntie talked to us as she took off her shoes and entered the living area.

Father came out of the room, and Auntie stared at his red eyes and then his back as he walked over to the rose garden with his cigarette. Auntie went into the room. We could hear Grandmother explaining something in a low voice, and Auntie saying out loud, "I can't take the boy, not even for a week—look what Sungjin did to him!"

PART II

The
Sea

 The Trip

On August fifteenth, a national holiday celebrating Korea's emancipation from Japanese rule, we were to leave for our vacation. A few days before, it was decided that we weren't going to our usual vacation spot but to a new place called Manlipo. Father wasn't talking to anyone since the evening he yelled at Grandmother and cried, and we hardly saw him. When he was home, Grandmother took over some of Mother's chores, bringing in his barley tea herself and even ironing his uniform. At first Father acted like he didn't notice any of Grandmother's goodwill gestures, but then slowly he began to yield to her.

Grandmother said that her friends, the Kangs, had a small beach house on the west coast, and that she thought a vacation at a new place would do him some good. Father softened a little and agreed that he wouldn't mind getting away from his colleagues for a while.

Usually, to prepare for a vacation, Mother bustled around and did five things at once. She sautéed the dried anchovies and heated the hot-pepper paste on the stove, stirring them occasionally, while oiling the seaweed to be salted and roasted, even as she instructed Soonja Uhnni to mend our clothing and not to forget to pack our bathing suits. Mother didn't have to look up; she knew when Soonja Uhnni was waiting for new chores. Sometimes she even knew what Soonja Uhnni wanted to ask and answered her before she opened her mouth. When we asked her a question, she stopped oiling the seaweed, walked over to the stove to check the rice for lunch, answered our question, stirred the anchovies and hot-pepper paste, then went back to oiling the seaweed.

But that summer, she forgot about the fish on the stove and cut her index finger while preparing lunch. Soonja Uhnni kept asking what she should do next, and Mother didn't hear us when we asked her a question. We were leaving in a day, but she was not close to being ready.

Changhee Uhnni and I laid out our own clothes to be packed, and Grandmother helped Moonhee and Keehee. This was the first year Keehee was old enough to come with us. She was so excited that she walked around the house making comments on the weather in the same way Grandmother had that morning, "Fair weather for traveling. The sea will be calm. Fair weather for traveling."

I tried to help Mother by taking care of Pyungsoo

that morning. I washed his face with a wet towel and fed him breakfast. Although he no longer had a bandage on the side of his face, he was weak and moved awkwardly with his right arm in the cast. Pyungsoo looked at us enviously, which made me feel guilty.

"What do you want me to bring back? Shells? Pebbles?" I asked him.

He was silent for a while.

"I don't even know what it looks like."

"You don't know what shells look like or what pebbles look like?"

"I never saw the ocean." Pyungsoo's ears reddened.

"I'll bring back everything. I'll even bring back the sand," I assured him.

Pyungsoo smiled sadly.

With Mother's cut finger she had to stay up late to get everything ready. On the morning of our departure, she went to a beauty salon to get her hair done and came back with a pretty twist, but she looked tired.

When we were ready, Grandmother followed us out and reassured us that she would take care of Pyungsoo and the house, but she sounded like she really wanted us to worry about everything. Pyungsoo stayed in Soonja Uhnni's room, and when I said good-bye, he avoided my eyes, so I left my only ten won next to him. It was the first ten won I had earned to pay back our helper for the toy soldier.

Father's military jeep took us to the harbor where we were to take a ship to Manlipo, which was at the tip of the western side of the peninsula. Father sat in front with the driver and didn't say much. Mother and the four of us, squeezed in the back, felt the sharp bumps of the road. Keehee, who was sitting on Mother's lap, looked out the window and then turned to us to see if we had any comments about the big bright bus or the tall buildings. But unlike other years when we couldn't stop chattering, we just sat quietly. Moonhee, who often got car sick, started to lean on my shoulder.

Our driver left us at Inchon harbor with our bags, and none of us moved for a little while. It was humid and muggy, as it often was in the middle of August, and Moonhee squinted into the hazy sun and threw up on the ground. Mother poured out some water into her handkerchief and wiped Moonhee's face.

Father left us to buy the tickets. When he returned, we followed him onto the big old ship, which smelled of salt and fish. Every time we took a step, the floor boards creaked under our feet, and it felt as though the sky moved slightly up and down.

In the main room other families had already claimed their spaces with picnic blankets. Mother took out ours and spread it in the corner next to the window that looked out on the sky.

A woman near us with her two sons smiled at us. "Four daughters? So many."

Mother pretended she didn't hear the woman and rearranged our bags. As soon as we were settled, Moonhee lay her head on Mother's leg and Mother stroked her back. Keehee, who hardly ever got sick, was already hungry, but Mother motioned for her to wait.

Father said he was going out to the deck to look around, and Changhee Uhnni and I followed him. We walked behind him, squeezed among the people milling about either to look out into the ocean or to find places to sit. Some people had brown skin from being out in the sun too much and spoke with a heavy accent. They were probably either farmers or fishermen going home after having visited Seoul. When Father stopped to get some cigarettes, we noticed a few male students who sat on the ledge of the railing with their feet hanging outside the ship. The elders around us whispered that they had no manners.

On the ocean side of the ship Father stopped to light his cigarette. We watched him cupping his hands around the lighter against the wind. After a few minutes, the ship made a loud roar and slowly left the harbor, parting the water like Mother parts my hair, smooth and tingly.

"How long is the trip, Father?" I had to speak loudly to fight the sound of the wind and water.

"Four hours." Father puffed the smoke in the air and it disappeared.

"Where is our old vacation place from here?"

"It's on the other side of the peninsula."

"Is Manlipo as nice as there?"

"All beaches are the same." Then Father changed his mind. "Maybe it will be less crowded."

I felt sorry for him ever since the night he cried, but I couldn't think of anything funny to say.

"I'm cold." Changhee Uhnni shivered.

"You go in first." Father motioned us toward the door.

"I'm not cold." I wanted to stay outside with him, but Father told us both to go in.

At the door I looked back, and Father stood there with the back of his shirt flapping in the wind. He looked smaller out of his uniform.

After a long nap I went outside. Standing next to Father, I looked at the water churning around the ship, then at the horizon that didn't seem to be moving at all. Little rocky islands appeared and disappeared, indicating how fast we were going. Father pointed, and I saw a strip of green land behind the shimmer of the air. It grew larger until we could see the divide between the dark blue water and the sandy shore with green hills behind it. People began to stir around us, and with a man's bellow and the loud horn, the ship slowly came to a stop.

"Tell everyone to get ready to leave," Father ordered.

"But we are in the middle of the ocean. How are we getting there?" I asked.

"A boat will come and pick us up."

As people moved forward, we saw the wooden ladder lowered on the side of the ship. On the water below were a few small boats huddling around it. A crew member helped people down the ladder while a dark-skinned man on one of the little boats held on to it.

Everyone had to face the ship and climb down. Some men jumped off the last step, making the boat rock and women scream, and other men looked a little scared. Some women lowered themselves gingerly, but the last step to the small boat was a big one, and they just hung on to the ladder until the boat owner yelled for them to let go. When it was our turn, Father handed our bags to the boat owner and got onto the boat first, then took Moonhee and Keehee as they were lowered in the air to him.

Changhee Uhnni climbed down next, then I followed her, and Father lifted us off the last step. Mother tried to climb down with one hand holding her skirt and then hesitated on the last step. Father stooped and helped her by supporting her back. We waited for a few more people to fill the boat, and then our boat owner rowed us toward the shore.

People commented on how beautiful the land looked from there and how the salt water cleared their noses and hearts. We could feel the water splash on our arms, and the muggy weather of Seoul seemed to have completely disappeared. The small white waves on the deep blue water bubbled and dissolved, and the light playing on the surface looked like stars. When we were close to the shore, the boat owner jumped in the waist-high water and towed us onto the land. We took off our shoes and let Father lift us out. Mother held on to Father's hand to step out of the boat.

CHAPTER 15

Father's Stew

When we felt the wet sand between our toes, our vacation began. The ocean looked large and friendly and the cool wind on the ship was now warm and breezy. Keehee, who was seeing the ocean for the first time, smiled happily, deepening both of her dimples. Even Moonhee's face lit up, showing her two missing teeth.

While some people walked away with their bags, others were greeted by people they knew. A tanned man in a straw hat and wearing a jacket and pants made of hemp approached us.

"Colonel Lee?"

"Yes, are you from Mr. Kang's?" Father asked.

"It's a pleasure to meet you for the first time." The man spoke politely with a heavy accent. "Let me take your luggage." He took a couple of bags, although Father protested that we could manage them ourselves.

We followed him up the sand dunes and then a grassy

hill. Mother asked polite questions about Mr. Kang's family, and he said they had weathered the *changma* well.

At the top of the hill, the man stopped in front of a beach house that looked like a box. It was made from gray concrete with a flat roof, and there were no walls surrounding the grounds.

The man said, "Mr. Kang asked me to tell you it's not much of a place but it's close to the water."

We turned around, and the view was breathtaking. The little hill we had climbed stretched before us, turning into sand dunes and at the bottom to sparkling water.

"I bought some fish and vegetables and local rice for you. It's under the shade." He pointed to the big tree next to the beach house.

Mother and Father thanked the man, and with a deep bow he left, saying he would come back three days later to help us down to our boat. But we couldn't imagine three days later, as if it had nothing to do with us.

In the yard there was a small makeshift stove made of rocks. Inside it were pieces of blackened wood that were not completely burnt. Three steps away stood an old-fashioned water pump, and next to it a tree stump with a few pieces of wood and an ax. Against the wall of the house, charred pots, a kettle, a kerosene burner, a wooden table, a pail, and a broom were lined up. In a small box near the broom, eating utensils stuck out.

While Father continued to survey the grounds, Mother went into the boxlike house. The beach house had two small rooms separated by a hallway. In each room was a wooden chest filled with pillows and blankets and insect incense. Mother took out the blankets and hung them on the branches to be aired and sunned. Moving fast, Mother seemed to be in a better mood. She brushed back her hair with her wrist, looked at the water, then went back into the house. She unpacked the food and put the jars and containers on top of the chest so the ants couldn't get to them. When Changhee Uhnni and I smelled the food, all of a sudden we were very hungry. We hadn't eaten anything on our trip because we were seasick, and now it was close to dinnertime.

As if Mother read our minds, she called out, "Father, please start the fire."

Father peered in. "Start the fire? In the stove?"

"What about the kerosene burner? By the time the rice is ready, it will be almost dinnertime." Mother hadn't asked anything of Father since the night he cried.

Changhee Uhnni and I came out of the house. We saw Father jiggle the rusty kerosene burner, but he couldn't get it to work.

"Go and gather some kindling," he ordered.

We just stared at him. We didn't know exactly what he wanted.

"Get twigs, sticks, dried leaves, branches, anything that will burn."

We spread out among the pine trees, which cast long shadows. I picked up pine cones, broken branches, and dried weed stems. Whenever I looked up, I was surprised and happy to see the water sparkle. Nearby, Moonhee was collecting shells, not twigs, and Keehee was chasing after the grasshoppers in the dunes. Only Changhee Uhnni seemed to be searching hard to find the best kindling to present to Father. When we got back with our collection, Father was chopping some wood. He put the ax carefully in the middle of the piece, tapped with a rock to split it open, then pounded the wood all the way down.

"Watch this," he said.

He brought the pieces of split wood with him to the stove he had already cleaned. We all squatted around him. He set down the dried stems first, the twigs, then branches. Last he put the big pieces of wood on top in a tent shape. He took out the steel lighter and lit the dried stems on the bottom, which quickly caught fire. Mother came and stood behind him and watched the flames ride up. Father didn't move at all, but the slight tension in his shoulders showed how close she was to him.

As Father got up he said, "It will be ready in fifteen minutes."

Mother stared at the fire as Father walked away. Then she went over to wash the rice in the iron pot. She measured the water by putting her hand into the pot. When the water came up around her knuckles she put in a little more.

All of us sat on the straw mat and waited for the fire to be ready. Mother turned toward the ocean, and it seemed her face was lit up by the reflection on the water. She had changed into a sleeveless pale green poplin shirt and midlength skirt with a little lavender flower print. She looked pretty even though she didn't think so. Mother didn't like certain things about her looks—her high-bridged nose, the vaccination marks on her upper right arm, and the big scar on her left knee. But most of all, she didn't like her big feet. She often said she was glad none of us had her feet.

They didn't look so big to me except when we went to buy shoes. Then the lady standing among many pairs of shoes often said she didn't have Mother's size.

"Such a big size," she said. "Wear a size smaller and your feet will look small."

Sometimes Mother did buy a size smaller. I could see how uncomfortable she was in those shoes by the way she walked around with a slight wince. Mother was even careful not to line up her shoes next to Grandmother's.

Mother stretched her legs and rubbed her knee. The scar under the skirt was shaped like the gaping mouth of an alligator. Fifteen years ago she had fallen into a big open hole full of sharp pebbles and dirt. She said that was the only time she cried as an adult because of physical pain, but we saw her cry sometimes for other reasons.

Lying on my side next to Mother, I saw Father by the dunes bending down to pick up something. Through the arch his body made I saw a little boy running on the beach. I thought about Pyungsoo and felt badly for him, but it was good to be just us. Father stood up and turned in our direction. I couldn't see his face from all the light behind him, but I thought he might be looking at Mother. When he climbed back up he checked the fire.

"What kind of soup are we having?" he asked.

"I thought maybe we could skip soup and just eat rice and the fish that man left. We still have the lunch we didn't eat," Mother said.

"Today, I'll make some fish stew," Father announced, and we were very surprised.

"Father, you know how to make fish stew?" I asked.

"What ingredients do we have?" Without answering me he went over to the bag the man had left and peered in. He pulled out a shiny mackerel, green scallions, a cabbage, and a turnip. Mother got up quickly and brought out jars of soybean paste and hot-pepper paste from inside the house.

We got up and walked over to the water pump. As Mother washed the food and handed it to him, she looked like she was biting down a smile. Father took everything to the tree stump and cut the scallions, cabbage, and turnip into small pieces and put them in a bowl. Then he scaled the fish in even strokes, sliced its stomach, carefully pulled out the insides, and cut the fish into four.

"Save the head," Mother said. "It's the best part."

"How do you know how to make fish stew, Father?" I asked again.

This time Mother, who had been watching with us, answered for him.

"Your father knows how to make rice, stew, and even *kimchee* well."

"Don't give them the wrong impression." Father liked to be precise about everything, even what he did badly. "I learned to make bad food for hundreds of people at the Military Academy when I started."

Father put the pot with water on the stove. He stirred in some soybean paste and hot-pepper paste, added the vegetables, and covered the pot. The way Mother made stew was to let the water boil before putting vegetables in, but she didn't say anything.

"We made rice without washing out most of the stones."

"What else can you make?" Moonhee asked him.

"*Kimchee*, you can't possibly imagine how we made it. We put on rubber boots to step on the cabbages to mix in the spices."

We all laughed. We couldn't imagine our father in a uniform with rubber boots walking on cabbages.

"Where did they put that much cabbage?" I asked.

Father smiled. "In a huge bathtub."

"A bathtub?" we all said at the same time.

"Those big communal bathtubs," he said. "They cleaned it. It doesn't matter. You can't possibly imagine how life is for men, especially in the military. If you don't eat fast enough you don't even get the rice with stones. Someone sitting next to you will take it from you."

I thought about how slowly he ate.

"When I was pregnant with Junehee"—Mother looked at me—"I had no helper, and your father sometimes made rice and bean sprout soup for us. That was a hot summer when I carried you, very hot. Sweat rolled down my face just sitting in the shade. When the cool breeze came, you were born."

I was glad that Father made meals for Mother when she was pregnant with me.

Mother continued, "In the small kitchen, your father just wore underwear when he made dinner."

We laughed.

"Do you remember that house?" Mother asked Father.

Father nodded while digging the ground next to the tree stump to bury the fish guts.

"That's over ten years ago. They say even rivers and mountains change completely in ten years. People must change more than that." Mother's tone turned a little sad.

Father still didn't say anything, and Mother got up. She unfolded the legs of a wooden table, wiped it with a wet dish towel, and put it in the middle of the straw mat. She laid out the various side dishes we brought and put out the box lunches she had prepared for our trip. There was plenty of everything—pickled salty turnip, seasoned lotus roots, crispy seaweed, roasted dried anchovies, marinated beef cubes, and *kimchee*. I put out the chopsticks and spoons. When the stew and rice were ready, Changhee Uhnni scooped the rice from the pot. Mother told her to gently fluff up the rice first. That way, she said, it didn't all clump together.

The stew pot sat in the middle of the table to be shared. We all commented on how delicious Father's stew was. It wasn't as rich as Mother's, but it still tasted good. Mother took the head of the fish, and Changhee Uhnni and I asked for the eyeballs. We liked the soft outer layer and the chewy inside. It felt strange and wonderful to eat outdoors, looking at the ocean and feeling the breeze.

 # Sea Wind

After dinner we watched Mother clean the pots. She twisted and knotted tall dried weeds into a scouring pad, rubbed the pots hard with water and ash, and they turned shiny in her hands.

The sun began to move slowly toward the horizon as we finished cleaning.

"*Yeobo*, should we go and walk in the sea wind?" Mother often called Father *Yeobo*, dear, when Grandmother wasn't around. In front of Grandmother she called him Father as we did.

Father was standing with a cigarette in his hand. He didn't turn around. He just adjusted the belt on his pants, as was a habit with him, then continued to stare at the ocean.

Mother talked to his back. "We can see the sunset, not sunrise, here."

At the military officers' resort we got up early to see the sunrise.

Father, without answering, put on his hat, which hung on the tree branch, and set out for the dunes. He meant for us to follow him. Mother scurried around looking for her sandals and we put on our thongs, then quickly walked down the beaten path we had come up several hours before. We could hardly keep our eyes on the water because the sun was moving closer to the horizon. Instead we looked down and saw long green flying insects hiding in the weeds.

When we got down to the sandy shore, we turned right and headed toward the green hill that jutted out into the water, creating an inlet. Only a few people strolled and swam at that time. Usually Father walked ahead alone while Mother kept pace with us. But that evening Mother caught up with him, leaving us to follow them. We took off our thongs and carried them, letting the water come up on our feet. It felt good when with each step the receding waves left our feet sunken in the sand. Keehee and Moonhee walked beside me, and Changhee Uhnni behind us. As always, she was quiet when Father was around.

The seagulls flew low and landed on the sand not too far away from us. I heard Mother mentioning how the sand in Manlipo was finer and darker than in Book-pyung. Mother wasn't using polite language with Father. I listened to her against the sound of seagulls moving like waves, rising and falling.

"*Yeobo*, do you remember that beach?" Mother asked.

Father turned and I could see he had no idea. We had to be very specific when we asked him questions.

"The beach in Pusan," Mother clarified. Father then nodded a little. "The waves were going *chul-lung, chul-lung* in that deep blue sea."

We loved the way Mother made just the right sound for certain things. She knew the sound of waves just as well as the sound of rain. *"Ji-kul, ji-kul,"* she would say for rain. When we said that sounded like fire crackling, Mother told us to close our eyes, and it did sound just like rain coming down.

Mother could mimic people, by copying the sound they made every time they finished a sentence or imitating the way they lifted one eyebrow or the way they stuck out their lips. It was easy to visualize the person's face when watching her. She also described food so well our mouths watered at the thought of juicy persimmons bursting their skins, chestnuts being roasted on the streets, or chewy zucchini taffies turning soft as we pulled them apart.

Mother continued, "The shells rolled *dhing-kool, dhing-kool* from the wind. It was so cold."

"I don't remember," Father said.

"You picked up the shells for me. That was the last time I saw Pusan." After a moment of silence Mother asked, "Do you remember how you used to come up to Seoul from there?"

"When?"

"Why, *Yeobo*, if someone else were listening to us they would think our marriage was arranged. Right after we were engaged. Don't you remember? You were transferred to Pusan."

"Hm." Father just grunted.

"Mother used to kill a chicken every time you came up," Mother said.

I could imagine Grandma Min chasing down a chicken to serve her future son-in-law.

"Except that time. You came up twice in one day. Mother only had one chicken to kill and she had already served you."

"Twice, in one day, from Pusan?" Father looked at her incredulously.

"Your friend, the one in the air force, flew you up in the morning, then you flew back up with him in the afternoon when you found out there was another delivery coming back to Seoul."

"Father, do you remember that?" I regretted asking the question as soon as the words came out of my mouth. I didn't want them to think I was eavesdropping.

Mother turned toward us. "My mother ran out without her shoes because she thought something terrible had happened. She still talks about that now."

We walked silently for a while until we came to the rocky area of the jutting land. We sat on flat dry rocks.

"I kept the shells from that beach for a long time," Mother said.

Father looked at Mother with that blank expression. With Father we often had to explain from the beginning to the end, but Mother could pick up a word from a conversation and know what the entire story was about.

"Mother, do you still have them?" Moonhee asked her.

"No, I lost them in the move. I just have the letters."

"Letters from me?" Father asked.

"*Yeobo*, who else . . ." Mother paused a little, then with her clever smile said, "I only kept yours."

That made Father smile.

We saw the sun become a half circle behind the horizon, then disappear quickly.

That night we went to sleep in a good mood. Mother left a little candle in our room so we wouldn't be afraid. Without the candle the place was pitch black because there was no electricity. We lay on the straw mattress and watched the thin smoke of the burning mosquito incense go up to the ceiling. There wasn't any glass in the square space cut out for a window and the breeze made the smoke dance.

Changhee Uhnni crawled over to the candle dish that Mother had put on the top of the chest. She wanted to make animal shadows on the wall with her hands.

"Mother said not to move the candle." I was afraid Changhee Uhnni would tip it over.

"Be quiet," she ordered, and slid the candle dish toward her.

"Look." Changhee Uhnni put her hand in front of the flame and made a chicken shape on the wall. She flapped her hands like wings. We looked. "I know how to make a rabbit too," she said, and maneuvered her hands. But the new shape didn't look like a rabbit.

"That's not a rabbit," Keehee blurted out.

"It is too. Look." She tried again.

Keehee was lying on her side with her head propped up. She shook her head.

"What do you know. You are only six." Changhee Uhnni sat up and towered over us.

"I know what a rabbit looks like," Keehee insisted.

"Don't be stupid, you don't know what anything looks like. You don't even go to school."

"I know how to write my name."

"I know how to write everyone's name." Changhee Uhnni was still trying to make a better rabbit with her hands.

"Children," Mother warned from the next room.

"See? Be quiet." Changhee Uhnni made Mother's scary eyes by opening hers wider. Then she mouthed, "Watch." She lay back and started writing everyone's name in the air with her finger. She wrote Grandmother's, Father's, Mother's, and ours.

When she finished she smiled triumphantly.

"What about Pyungsoo Opa's name?" Keehee asked softly.

Changhee Uhnni glared at her, and the candle flame swirled in her eyes. Keehee turned away as though she didn't mean to say it.

"He isn't a member of our family. He's an orphan and his name doesn't count."

"Park Pyungsoo," I whispered his name slowly.

She narrowed her eyes. "I'm going to tell Mother about the math test, and the comic books, and when you played flower cards with Sungjin."

I didn't say anything after that. I didn't know she knew about the comic books and playing the flower cards.

I listened to the distant waves, wondering how I was going to bring some sand home for Pyungsoo. First I had to find an empty jar. I thought about which jar of side dishes we would finish first, the roasted minnows? Hot-pepper paste? Then I thought of putting the sand in my sock. . . .

I was awakened by the sound of waves becoming louder and louder, but when I opened my eyes, all I heard was a creaking noise. The room was pitch black and it seemed as though my eyes were still closed. Then I remembered we were at Manlipo and closed my eyes, wanting it to be morning soon so I could go to the beach. I heard whispering.

"I am not as strong as you think," Mother said.

"You are stronger than I am," Father said.

It sounded like Mother's and Father's words were bouncing off each other's faces.

"Why don't you depend on me a little, then?" Mother spoke softly.

"I am a man."

"Yes," Mother sighed. "But I can see you feel worse in the mornings after all that drinking."

Father cleared his throat.

Mother continued, "I know I have little right as an outsider. I haven't asked you for anything. Of course it's not my place." Mother was talking faster. "Anyway, what would complaints do? I accept my lot and do what I can. When our daughters leave us there will be no one for us. I accepted that fate, but then God sent us this boy."

"What God?" Father said in a mean tone. "The boy came into our house because they were poor and had a straw-thatched house up on the mountain where there were no trees to hold the ground, because we live in a poor country."

Mother continued as though she didn't hear him. "Our house isn't that big but it's big enough, and we can feed another mouth. I think with time you may come to accept the boy. He is traumatized but he is bright and he has a good *insang*."

"You hope to have a son based on your assessment of *insang*? Did you study face reading?" Father's words were sharp.

I tried to imagine exactly how Pyungsoo's face looked.

"He can go to school with Changhee and Junehee. I will make his uniform, and he can sleep with your mother." Mother didn't give up as she usually did.

Father's voice rose. "No."

Mother didn't say anything more for a while.

When she spoke again she sounded sad. "If only there had been an incubator." I wondered what an incubator was.

"Dr. Chae said if there had been an incubator my boys could have lived. There are so many now. Only one, there was only one then."

"Don't talk about that anymore," Father said firmly to Mother, but she didn't stop.

"Both times I felt babies kicking my thighs. The midwife said they were boys. I had two boys."

"Erase that from your memory."

"I had two boys."

"You don't know how to forget things."

I couldn't fall asleep even though they had become quiet. I would have had two older brothers if only they had had an incubator, some kind of medicine that made babies well, I thought. Mother could have had two sons. I imagined Pyungsoo older than me, holding my hand and walking me down the main street to school. He would pat my head at the gate before saying good-bye.

CHAPTER 17
Other Women

The next morning Mother rubbed olive oil on our bodies, and we spent the whole day running in and out from under the blue beach umbrella she guarded. Mother had on her flowery bathing suit under the green dress that she didn't take off all day. Father walked around with his hat on for a while in the morning, but came into the shade complaining that his shoulders were getting burnt.

Even though Mother and Father squeezed together under the umbrella to avoid the sun, they didn't say much. At breakfast I noticed Mother's swollen eyes. When we came to the beach, she tried to be cheerful, saying things like, "How wide and beautiful this beach is, it makes my heart open up," but when she thought no one was watching, she stared sadly into the water.

Father had his mouth tightly closed, and he didn't

show us how to swim as he had done on our other vacations. Changhee Uhnni and Moonhee splashed in the shallow water with rubber tubes around them. Keehee and I sat by the shoreline and stuffed small bowls with sand and turned them upside down. From there I could watch everyone if I just turned my head.

Mother and Father's mouths moved. I knew they were talking about something unpleasant by the way Mother frowned and Father turned his head away from her. I could only hear parts of the conversation after a wave broke and receded into the sea and before the next one crashed.

"I have so little," Mother said.

Father looked away with a wince.

I heard "I," "trapped animal," "your sister," "everything," "the only thing"—then a wave broke.

Father stared at Mother with a mocking smile.

"Only this I will ever ask of you. Your mother will listen . . ." Mother's words were drowned in the sound of the waves.

Father didn't say anything but got up, brushed the sand off his legs, and walked away from Mother toward the green hill on the other side of the inlet. Mother rocked back and forth with her arms around her knees.

By lunchtime Father hadn't returned, and we ate without him. We took a nap and played in the water some more, and finally packed our things and walked up the dunes. Without Father, Mother had to carry more bags.

"Why isn't Father here yet?" Moonhee asked timidly.

"He is looking around," Mother answered.

"But he has been gone for a long time. What is he looking for?" she asked.

Mother didn't answer her as she continued to climb up the hill. Her face was red even though she had sat under the umbrella most of the day, which made her look angry. Mother didn't get very angry often, but when she did, especially if it was because of us, we were very scared.

Usually she just watched us. Then when one of us did something very bad, like lie to her, she scolded all of us for everything we had done wrong for months. She remembered the time when I stormed out of Grand-mother's room because she called me clumsy, when Changhee Uhnni hurt our helper's feelings by calling her a lowly servant, and when Moonhee ignored Kee-hee's questions.

Mother would say with her scary eyes, "It must be my fault that my children can think of being rude to their elders and to someone below their class, and even to a younger sister."

"Junehee." She would look at me. "You went over to your friend's house when you told me you were at school. I must not have done my duty as a mother." Then she hit us on the backs of our legs. We cried and promised we would never do it again.

But once in a while when she gathered us together, she was furious. Her face was very red and she breathed hard.

"What have I to live for in this house? What is there for me? How could you disappoint me like this?" Mother got angrier and angrier with every word she spoke. "Still, I must be to blame."

Then Mother did what we hated most. She lashed her legs and arm with a switch that was intended for us. We could hear the whipping sound: *swish, swish.*

"There is nothing for me to live for. Nothing."

We cried out loud, "Mother, Mother, we'll never do it again."

We tried to hold her hand back so she couldn't hit herself anymore, but she would push us away and continue.

It was easier when she hit us.

Mother was silent as she poured the water on us. We usually loved this routine, when she washed off the oil and sand and we put on new clothes before dinner, but this time we were just as quiet as she was.

As we prepared dinner, I saw Father walking slowly up the hill.

Mother talked to him as though nothing was wrong. "Dinner will be ready in five minutes. Do you want me to pump some water for you?"

Father shook his head and drew his own water.

I once overheard Soonja Uhnni talking to a helper from the neighborhood. She said sometimes Father would come home early in the morning, and Mother would only say, "Come in, what would you like for breakfast? Would you like some hot water to wash?" with a smile on her face. Soonja Uhnni said Mother wasn't an average woman. She could endure.

Father didn't say one word during dinner, and when Mother asked him if he wanted more rice, he just shook his head. Right after dinner he sat on a tree stump and smoked until we went into the house to sleep.

That night I tried to stay up, but my eyelids were heavy with sleep. When I opened my eyes it was already morning.

Father wasn't anywhere when we came out of the house. Mother sat by the stove checking the rice.

"Where is Father?" I asked.

"He went fishing."

"When is he coming back?"

"Tomorrow."

"Tomorrow?"

"He went deep-sea fishing. The boat will bring him back tomorrow." Mother stirred the bean sprout soup.

I was angry with myself for not staying up to listen to their conversation.

"We are going to eat breakfast, then go down to the beach. We may even buy some crabs or bean-cake ice cream if a vendor shows up," Mother said determinedly.

But Mother didn't come in the water all day. She just sat under the umbrella and looked far away. We tried to behave well, but Changhee Uhnni took the bigger rubber tube and didn't share with us until Mother finally noticed. I pulled Keehee in the big rubber tube and Moonhee in the smaller one by the shallow water.

"Mother, the water is cool. Come in," I shouted, but she just nodded and smiled.

I felt the hot air around me, and the salt dried too quickly on my face, leaving my skin stiff. I let go of Keehee and Moonhee and waded over to Changhee

Uhnni, who had gotten bored without her tube and was trying to body surf.

"Do you know why Father went fishing?" I asked. Sometimes she knew things I didn't just because she was older.

"Father got tired of you." She answered too quickly which showed that she didn't know anything. Then she surprised me. "He doesn't want Mother to adopt that stupid orphan. Too bad." She stuck out her tongue.

"How do you know that?"

She smiled slyly. "What are you going to give me if I tell you?"

I hesitated. I didn't want to show her how much I wanted to find out. She would take all the good things I have, but it was too late.

"How about your fish coin purse?"

"No! I just got that."

"Forget it." She turned away.

"I'll give you my ant ring."

The transparent ring that had a dead ant in the middle was given to me by Mother's cousin. He brought one back from Brazil for each of us, but Changhee Uhnni had lost hers. It was the third-best possession I owned, next to the sequined fish coin purse and the necklace with a cross that had a small lens in the middle with the Lord's Prayer written in Italian. Our priest-uncle gave these to us.

Changhee Uhnni narrowed her eyes to think about it, then said, "No, I want the coin purse."

"I can't give you that."

"Then forget it."

"I'll give you the ant ring and my portion of choco-late the next time we get some."

She thought about it and then put out her pinkie. "Promise." I shook it with my pinkie.

"I heard them last night."

"What did they say?"

"Father said absolutely not. He said he didn't even want to talk about it. Then Mother said . . ." Changhee Uhnni hesitated.

"What? You promised, Uhnni."

"I want the fish coin purse for this."

"No, you promised!"

"Oh, all right," Changhee Uhnni acted as though she were being generous. "Mother said she doesn't care if Father has other women as long as she can have the boy, but Father said no."

"Other women? What other women?" In the background I saw Mother looking at the green hills where Father had disappeared to the day before.

"Why do you think Father is late every night?" Changhee Uhnni asked.

"I don't know. He goes out with his friends."

"Where do you think they go?"

"To drink rice wine?"

"Who do you think they drink with?"

"I don't know, who?"

"Those bad women."

"What bad women?"

"Figure it out for yourself." Changhee Uhnni floated on her back and paddled away.

I went over by Mother and sat for a while and thought more about the other women. On television I saw how some men drank with bar girls, but I thought the women only poured drinks.

Mother took out a camera and started to take pictures

of Moonhee and Keehee in the water. One of her relatives had given her an old Canon camera and she took pictures of us when Grandmother and Father weren't around.

"I can do what I please," Mother muttered as she clicked away.

"Junehee, come sit where I am." Mother moved out from under the umbrella and sat in the sun. "Let's see what I look like at thirty-eight."

When I sat where she was, Mother stepped back and looked at me through the camera. She turned the black knob this way and that way and then dug her feet in the sand.

"You stand here and just push this button." She showed me the shiny silver button in the top right-hand corner. I stood exactly where she had marked with her feet, and she sat out in the sun where I had been.

Through the lens I saw Mother smiling. The wrinkles around her eyes seemed deeper in the sun and she showed her gums by stretching her mouth too widely. She leaned back on her arms with her legs stretched out in front of her. If Father saw her he would have said to tuck her legs under her so they didn't seem as big.

Around lunchtime, a vendor carrying a big basin on her head came along, shouting, "Hot crabs!" After bargaining with the woman for a few large crabs, Mother offered her some of our lunch.

"Don't mind if I do." The old woman didn't hesitate, and sat down with us. She showed us how to eat crabs while complaining about her two sons who had left for Seoul to look for jobs two months ago. They hadn't written to her yet.

As she shoved rice into her mouth, the woman said, "What good are sons if they forget their own mother?" She glanced at us. "They sure are pretty and healthy— good girls, aren't they? Yes, daughters are better than sons. I have one, she waits for me with dinner every night. Daughters are better, yes." Then without looking at Mother, the woman stuck out her bowl for more rice.

"If I die," she said, "I'm going to give my gold tooth to my daughter, not my sons." The woman had one gold tooth that shone against her wrinkled brown face.

Mother asked how she came to have a gold tooth.

"My husband drank with the little money I made selling crabs. One day I decided to put it where he couldn't use it. Just to make him angry I used to smile at him all the time."

Mother laughed.

The woman finished eating, and she gave us a few extra crab legs. Mother handed her a yellow melon, telling her to bring it to her daughter. She walked away wiping her eyes, mumbling something about *chung* between strangers.

After lunch we lay around our mother. She sang us our favorite lullaby, "Our Baby, Pretty Baby." I stretched out under the umbrella with my feet sticking out in the sun and wondered if Father had caught any fish.

When I woke up from the nap, I just lay in the shade and watched the heat rise from the hot sand. It danced in front of the green hill and the people and the umbrellas. Far away behind a young man kicking a soccer ball, I saw a small but familiar figure walking our way. He carried two long poles and had on a blue hat with a brim all around. I waited without saying anything. I wanted everyone to be surprised, especially Mother. But when the man came closer I saw that the hat didn't look like Father's after all.

CHAPTER 18

 Mother's Fingers

Father didn't return the evening he was supposed to, and we spent another day on the beach without him. All day I thought of those other women Changhee Uhnni mentioned. I tried to ask her more about them, but she wanted the fish coin purse. If they weren't bar girls, I thought, they might be like the singers who wore sequined dresses and sang on television, or like the actresses on the calendars with their slight smiles and small hands. I floated on my back, feeling the cool water and hot sun on my face, and wondered if those women felt the sea and the sun as I did.

Mother finally came in the water that day, and we let her use the tube. The only thing Mother did worse than we did was swim. Even though she loved the water, she only knew how to do the dog paddle. Moonhee and I hung on to her tube and kicked our feet. Mother let the tube carry us to the deeper water and then brought us back to the shallows. We took turns with Keehee and Changhee Uhnni.

No one mentioned Father, but each of us looked to the green hill from time to time when we thought Mother wasn't watching.

That evening after a dinner of leftover *kimchee* stew and cold rice, we sat around the makeshift stove. The stew didn't take long to heat and the fire Mother started was still going strong. We only had one more meal to cook, the next day's breakfast, and Mother heaped on the remaining wood. Then she took out the ears of corn we had just bought at the beach. They were already boiled, so she put them on the grill to roast.

We were mostly quiet except Keehee, who loved to eat, especially corn. She squatted right next to the ears without taking her eyes off of them, asking often if they were done. Mother rolled them around with her bare hands. She never used a dish towel or her apron when touching most hot things. Mother could pick up a pot right off the stove, then hold her earlobes to cool her fingers.

But Mother did cut herself often in the kitchen, and that spring when I saw the white gauze on top of her hand, I asked, "Mother, did you cut your hand? What happened?"

Soonja Uhnni, who was behind Mother, looked at me and shook her head as though something were wrong and I shouldn't be asking the question.

"I cut it making breakfast," Mother said as she moved

to the sink to wash the dishes. Then she remembered about her hand. A few days later, she started to wash clothes and afterward changed the gauze in Soonja Uhnni's room.

When Mother wasn't around, I went in the kitchen and asked for a glass of water.

"You just drank barley tea," Soonja Uhnni snapped as she reached into the dish cabinet to bring out a glass.

"I'm thirsty."

"How can such a little body need so much water."

"Look." After drinking the water, I showed her a little paper cut I had on my index finger.

"It's nothing. I can't even see any blood."

"It still hurts."

"Put your saliva on it," Soonja Uhnni said.

"That won't make it better. That's just for mosquito bites."

She blew on my finger in her awkward way, with her lips protruding, and said, "It's all better now."

"Can't I have a little piece of gauze and tape?"

She looked at me, then turned her head.

"I don't have any."

"Yes, you do. It's in your room," I said.

"Ask your mother."

"Did you see the cut, Uhnni?"

Soonja Uhnni shook her head, but I knew she was lying.

"What happened to her hand?"

"You children should obey her better. You are all she has."

"I obey her," I said.

"Not you so much . . ." she admitted.

"Your mother, she has so much *han*," was all she said before waving me away.

If our helper thought Mother had so much *han*, then something was really wrong. Soonja Uhnni always said she had the most *han*—sorrow and regret—in this world. There she was, a poor girl with a sick father, no mother, and just one skirt. She would never get married and have children, she said, because she was born into an ill-fated family. No one in her family, not her grand-parents or great-grandparents, had ever even felt satin on their skin. They only wore rough cotton and ate barley rice. She always said that she had the most *han*.

After that I watched Mother closely and listened carefully to everything she said, but I still wasn't sure what Soonja Uhnni meant. The day the gauze came off, I sat next to Mother in church. She kneeled with her hands gathered for praying. I saw at close range a slightly discolored oval-shaped scar on the back of her hand. I had seen the marks before, but until then I didn't know what they were. They were teeth marks. I put my mouth on the top of the pew and tasted the wood with my tongue.

That scar from a few months past had almost disap-peared, except for two little dark marks near her thumb. They looked like the slightly burnt corn kernels she was scraping off the cob.

The evening breeze blew Mother's hair onto her face. She didn't bother putting it into a bun after she washed it. She had slightly wavy hair like her brother.

"Mother, you look young," I said.

"Young?" She smiled with her mouth closed, as though she had something bitter in it.

"Why don't you keep your hair down?" I asked.

"No, make it shorter like Mrs. Park's," Moonhee commented.

Mrs. Park had a short haircut with a teased top and a tapered back.

"Short?" Mother touched her hair, feeling the waves.

"Very short," I added. Mrs. Park was always smiling, and I could see Mother smiling in a short haircut.

"Your grandmother and father wouldn't like it."

"They never like anything," I said, faster than I meant to.

"Junehee," Mother scolded me gently.

"When is Father coming back? Tomorrow?" Moonhee asked.

"I guess before noon. We'll be leaving here then."

"Is Father angry with us?" Moonhee asked again.

"No."

All of us waited for Mother to tell us more, but she just turned over the corn she had rearranged and sat back. She looked at us and smiled sadly. "Your father is angry at me because I don't listen to him."

"Mother always listens to him." Even as I said that I knew that wasn't true. She said yes to everything but sometimes she went against him secretly, especially if it was for us.

In the winter of that year Mother enrolled Moonhee in an art class against Father's and Grandmother's wishes. Moonhee had just won an art contest and her friends who were also winners were going to after-school tutoring. When Mother mentioned it, Father said it was useful to be somewhat coordinated but to spend money was not a good idea. Grandmother agreed. Mother didn't say anything then, but two days later, she took Moonhee and enrolled her in the class.

"Isn't Father going to be angry?" I asked as Moonhee and I followed Mother up the steps to the studio.

"He doesn't see," was all she said.

Later that day, Mother explained to Father and Grandmother that Moonhee could take the art class for a very small fee, which Mrs. Park was giving her for her birthday. Grandmother just nodded and Father looked at Mother suspiciously, but Mother didn't change her expression at all.

The next day, I saw Mother taking out the twenty-four-karat gold band her mother had given her before getting married. She put in on her fourth finger and tilted her head this way and that way. Mother mumbled something about her fingers not being pretty anyway. She took off the ring, put it in her purse, and left the house. When she returned, she brought a box of our favorite cake for no particular reason at all. Grandmother seemed surprised, but she didn't ask her where she got it.

Mother gazed out into the sea and touched her face as though she hadn't felt it in a long time.

"Your father is right. I don't listen to him."

Changhee Uhnni, who had been quiet, said, "He left because Mother wanted to adopt the boy." She was poking the corn with her sticks and didn't look up.

Mother stared at her and spoke very slowly in her low, controlled tone. "In years to come, when you are a stranger in someone else's house and you have no one to speak with, you will understand that even your daughters are not your own. That you have no one."

"Whose daughters are we then? Even Mother doesn't want us." This time Changhee Uhnni stared boldly into Mother's eyes.

Mother turned her head, then in one quick, angry motion she pulled her hair back and made a bun by twisting the tail with her finger. She held the bun with one hand and with the other hand took a bobby pin out of her pocket, opened it against her teeth, and thrust it in the bun. Now she looked more like our mother.

"Am I not a daughter too? Do you think my mother loves me less than she loves my brother?"

"You still want the boy."

"Why do you think I want a son?"

Changhee Uhnni didn't answer. Mother reached over, grabbed Changhee Uhnni's hand and pulled her toward her. Changhee Uhnni looked scared but stood still. Mother took Changhee Uhnni's hand and put the thumb in her mouth and bit it, which made Changhee Uhnni scream out of fear. She tried to take her hand away, but Mother held it firmly and bit all five fingers one by one.

"Because," Mother said, "I can't bear that all my fingers will be cut away from me someday."

Changhee Uhnni stared at her fingers, then burst out crying.

Mother stood up slowly and walked toward the dunes, then plopped down on the ground. By the way she held her head in her hands, I knew she was also crying.

I took the burnt corn off the grill before bringing Moonhee and Keehee into the room and laying out the blankets.

"Be very quiet and go to sleep," I told them, and they got under the blankets.

I went out and waited for Mother to come and Changhee Uhnni to stop crying, but after waiting for a while I came back in and lay next to Moonhee.

Eventually Changhee Uhnni shuffled in and fell asleep rolled up in a ball. For a while I listened and waited for Mother to come in, but all I heard was water splashing outside. It sounded like Mother was washing things and getting ready for the next day's departure.

There were a few empty jars, but I hadn't collected any shells or sand for Pyungsoo. As I lay there I couldn't get the picture of his disappointed face out of my mind. I saw his eyes lowering and his large ears move in a funny way. Then I saw his excited eyes when he got the shells and grasshoppers. I saw Father's triangle eyes behind Pyungsoo's, Mother's sorrowful eyes, Changhee Uhnni with my ant ring, her fingers, Mother's wavy hair, babies kicking . . .

CHAPTER 19

The Ugly Man

I woke up abruptly to the sound of seagulls and for a while I couldn't figure out why I felt bad. Then I remembered. I put on my clothes quickly and stepped over Changhee Uhnni, who was still sleeping rolled up on her side. Outside Mother squatted by the stove doing something, but she looked strange. I walked over to her slowly and saw that her hair was messy and short, sticking out in all different directions. Mother lifted her head, smiling sheepishly.

"I have to go to a beauty salon when I go home. It didn't come out right," she said as she felt her hair.

"Mother, you cut your own hair?"

"I couldn't do the back too well," she answered.

But it wasn't just that the back was awful. It was all in clumps. Even the front was jagged, and when the wind blew the hair onto her face, she didn't look like our mother.

"Your father is going to be surprised." She turned away and continued cutting up the zucchini.

I went back to the room and told everyone that Mother cut her hair and not to be surprised, but I knew it was no use. Changhee Uhnni gave me a look and turned away, twisting her blanket around her body.

At breakfast Changhee Uhnni said she wasn't hungry and didn't eat with us. Moonhee and Keehee glanced at Mother's face often, but I didn't have to look to know what she had done to her hair.

We were all packed when Mr. Kang's friend came up. Even the man stared at Mother curiously, as if he noticed something different but didn't quite know what it was. Mother kept brushing her hair back as she talked with him. She thanked him for the fresh mackerel and vegetables and told him about the local crabs and corn we enjoyed. When the man asked where Father was, she said he went deep-sea fishing and was supposed to be back soon.

Mr. Kang's friend said that he knew what direction the fishing boats came from and walked over to the left side of the house. I stood next to him and squinted hard at the place where we had watched the sunset a few days before. There was no sign of Father, but the man said the fishing boats were often late and we should go down the hill to wait by the shore.

In the hot sun all of us filed behind the man with our bags. Mother, with both of her hands full, couldn't brush her hair back and shook her head to get the hair out of her eyes.

At the bottom of the hill the small wooden boats started to gather, and more and more people came toward us. Mother insisted that the man go home. She said she was sure Father would show up any moment. He agreed but left us saying he would find out about the fishing boat.

We waited with Mother—except for Changhee Uhnni, who stood by herself next to strangers. It was so hot I was sweating, and Moonhee squatted on the sand trying to hide from the sun. Keehee buried her hands in the wet sand and I had to clean them with Mother's handkerchief. Mother put her hand over her eyes and looked in the direction where the man went to find our father.

We heard a loud *ppp-ang* and saw the ship coming in from far away. The boatmen began to help the people get on.

"What if Father doesn't come back?" I asked.

Mother didn't answer me. She clamped down her lips so hard that her thick upper lip had many tiny wrinkles.

"There is only one empty boat left," I said as I saw two boats leaving and the last boat being filled.

"Throw the bags first," the boatman shouted at us.

"When is the next ship going back to Seoul?" Mother asked.

"In four days. Are you coming or not?"

Mother hesitated and repeated the words, "Four days."

"Well?" The boatman asked impatiently.

"Hold on, hold on," someone shouted from far away. We saw Mr. Kang's friend running toward us, waving. Behind him was Father, without his hat, running with two long fishing poles that were bending against the motion of his body.

"Toss me the bags," the boatman shouted again.

Mother threw the bags to him one by one. She lifted Keehee first, then Moonhee, and handed them to him. I was still staring at Father when Mother pushed me, and Changhee Uhnni followed after me. Mother didn't wait for Father but rushed onto the boat.

Father came to the boat, took off his shoes, and tried to climb into it with the poles, but they knocked against the side, and without looking at Mother he handed them to her. Mother held them carefully, as if they were rose stems with many fine thorns. When Father squeezed in next to the boatman, the man began to row us away from the shore. Seated side by side, Mother and Father bowed to Mr. Kang's friend, then looked out at the sea in opposite directions.

Father's face had gotten darker, which made him look thinner. He didn't seem to have caught any fish, not even a small one.

"Where is your hat, Father?" I asked.

"It flew away," he said regretfully, turning his face away from me.

As our boat neared the ship, people stirred, and the boatman had to tell them to sit still. We climbed up the same ladder we came down and then settled in the big room. Mother hadn't said one word to Father.

Father stood by her. "Where is—" He stopped in the middle of his sentence. He started again. "Where is . . . What happened to your . . . ?" He pointed at Mother's hair.

Mother turned away and ignored him.

"What happened to your hair?"

"I cut it," she said in her distant voice.

Father stared at her hair. "*Nachom*, what is Mother going to say?"

"It's my hair."

Father wagged his finger at Mother. "Why did you . . . It's . . . it's ugly. Do you know that?"

"What difference does it make if I'm ugly? Who would look at me?" she said bitterly. Other people glanced at us, even though Mother and Father spoke in low tones.

Father began to say something else but changed his mind and walked out of the room. Mother stared out the window. I thought about those "other women" whose hair was in a perfect shape and who laughed quietly, covering their mouths with their small hands.

I walked around the deck, away from Father, rubbing the few shells I had picked up that morning. I hadn't gotten the sand or anything else for Pyungsoo—only a few washed-out shells that had lost their pink and pearly luster. Moonhee tagged along behind me, then caught up with me and held my hand. We always hated going back home from our vacation, but this time it seemed worse.

We went up to the railing and watched the boat churning through the water. Manlipo was no longer in sight and all around us was dark blue water. As we stood looking out, a loud man came up from behind us and pushed Moonhee aside, making her fall off the ledge she was standing on and hit her chin on the railing. She started to cry.

I glared at the man with the greasy hair, who was talking to his friend.

"You pushed her."

"Uh? What, little girl?" he pointed his chin at me.

"She fell off. You hurt her. Can't you see you hurt her?"

"This little blabbermouth is telling me something," he said to his friend standing next to him.

"We were looking at the ocean," I said, trying not to shout.

"Looking at the ocean? How old are you? Get out of here." He motioned with his hand like he was sweeping us away.

"You pushed my sister!" I shouted. Moonhee stopped crying and pulled my shirt from behind.

The man scoffed at me with his ugly slivered eyes, then pushed my head with his big hand. "Get lost."

I fought his hand with my head but I slid back, and the man and his friend laughed.

"Mister, you are a bad person!" I shouted.

His big hand pushed my head again, this time more harshly. "Shut up before I dump you in the sea." Then he went back talking to his friend.

I stood there staring at the man's back for a long time, but he didn't even look to see if I went away. I felt tears coming down on my hot cheeks and walked away from them. Moonhee followed me as I kept going around the ship. An old woman who had been watching called us and gave us her spot by the railing, and patted my head.

"My chin doesn't hurt anymore. Does your head hurt, Uhnni?" Moonhee tried to console me.

I took out the shells from my pocket and threw them into the water one by one.

"What was that?"

"Nothing."

"Why did you throw away those shells?" Moonhee asked.

"I don't want them."

"We can make a necklace out of them."

"Who wants a stupid necklace?"

"I do," she said softly. "You can thread them together. It makes a funny little sound when you move. If you want, you can have my shells." Moonhee slid her hand in mine and I didn't feel so angry anymore.

I didn't have to tell Moonhee not to say anything to Mother about what had happened. Inside, Keehee was sleeping on Mother's lap and Changhee Uhnni slept away from both of them. Without moving her legs, Mother took out some peaches from a brown bag and handed them to us. When I bit into the peach, the corner of my mouth burned, and I felt a blister starting. I let Mother put some ointment on it, and afterward lay next to Moonhee and slept until the ship reached Seoul.

 The Arrival

It was dark by the time we arrived home. Before we knocked on our door, Father looked at Mother's hair one more time and shook his head, but Mother pretended she didn't see him. When Grandmother saw Mother's hair, she started to say something but changed her mind.

Between bringing in the bags and putting Keehee to bed, there was enough commotion to distract Grandmother from seeing what was wrong. In the living area Pyungsoo stood and followed me with his eyes, and I finally had to look at him. As Mother passed by him she patted his head and asked him how his arm was. Father went straight to his room without saying a word to him. Grandmother had prepared dinner for us, but none of us was hungry. We just washed and got ready to sleep.

Even though I was tired I couldn't fall asleep. Soonja

Uhnni came in with honey to put on my lips where the blister had gotten big and bubbly.

"What happened?" she asked. When I didn't answer she said, "You don't have to tell me. I can tell something happened." Then she went out.

Changhee Uhnni, who hadn't talked much to anyone since that morning, lay next to me, but I could tell she wasn't sleeping either.

"What is the worst thing that could happen to you?" she asked me.

"What?"

"What is the worst thing that could happen to you?" Once in a while when nobody was around she asked me questions like that.

"I don't know."

"If you lost your arm or something, would that be the worst?" she asked.

"Maybe legs would be worse. Someone has to carry you around all the time," I said.

"What about your nose?"

"How can you lose a nose?"

"I mean if you weren't born with it, like that girl." There was a girl in our neighborhood who we had heard only had two holes and no nose, but we had never seen her.

"No, you could probably still smell," I answered.

"Eyes?"

"Maybe."

"What if Star died?"

I hated the thought of our dog dying, but it wouldn't be the worst.

"What is the worst thing that could happen to you?" I asked her.

"I asked you first." This was what she said whenever she didn't want to answer. But then she said, "If someone took my strawberry sequined purse or my beaded necklace, that would be the worst. I would kill them." Then she turned around and went to sleep.

I stared at the ceiling. Even in the dark I could see the green leaf design on the papered ceiling. I remembered the worst thing that did happen to me. It was when I was in the second grade and Mother went into the hospital for surgery. That day I walked home with Changhee Uhnni from school feeling sad. Even though Mother told us an appendectomy was as simple as getting your tonsils out, it was the first time she was away from us. When we came home Soonja Uhnni handed each of us a letter. It was the first letter we received from her. My letter said,

> My compassionate daughter Junehee,
> Mother can always depend on you to take care of the little ones and to obey Grandmother and Changhee Uhnni. If you are awake when Father comes home, be his friend and sit with him through dinner. Only one thing worries me about you, and I know I can trust you not to worry me. You are too impatient with Grandmother. Be good and make me proud of you.

After my letter, I looked over Moonhee's.

> My gentle daughter Moonhee,
> It makes Grandmother very happy to sleep with you, and

your obedience makes me very proud. Keehee depends on you to be a little mother. Help her to put on her clothes and to take them off at night. Spend time with her as you have been. I depend on you.

When I was done, Moonhee took the letter and brought it to her chest. Keehee handed me hers and I read for her.

My loving daughter Keehee,
While Mother is away Moonhee will take care of you. You are a brave girl and you've never been frightened easily. You can sleep near Junehee. Draw something for Mother and show it to me when I come back. Mother will come back soon.

We were all feeling very sad.

"Let me see yours." Changhee Uhnni demanded.

"Only if you show me yours," I said. Reluctantly she made the trade. In her letter it said,

My smart daughter Changhee,
Mother knows that in your heart you always forgive everyone because you are good. While I'm away, be kind to everyone. Your sisters look up to you for leadership and you have to set a good example. I know you can do that for Mother. Be kind to Grandmother and Soonja.

Moonhee started to cry, and soon all of us were crying loudly, and for the whole week Mother was away we read her letters every day and cried. It felt like Mother was never coming back. I kept asking Grandmother why Mother didn't return in a few days as she had promised, and Grandmother said she'd be back soon.

Even after Mother came back, for a long time we feared she would go away again. She didn't want to show us her scar, but at the communal bath we saw the long, silvery, wormlike line across her lower stomach. Not until months later did we find out she had a tumor that was found to be harmless. If Mother ever wrote another letter to us, it would be the worst thing that could happen to me.

PART III

The Visits

CHAPTER 21

 Mother's New Hair

The morning after we returned from our vacation, the first thing I did was to tiptoe into Mother and Father's room, where Moonhee was sleeping. I shook Moonhee and she opened her eyes halfway.

I whispered in her ear, "Where are the shells?"

She blinked, then took her hand from under the blanket and pointed at the little bag she had taken on the trip. I brought it to my room. Inside were a plastic bag full of different kinds of shells and pebbles, and a jar filled with tiny black mussels and seawater. She even brought back a few pine cones. I took out a couple of white clam shells, a trumpet shell, and one big conch shell and put them aside.

I noticed that the morning air was cool and the white mist settled around the rose garden like the mornings at Manlipo, but here it meant autumn was near. I knelt to wash my face by the water pump, but before I got up Pyungsoo handed me a towel.

"You look like an African," Pyungsoo said. "What did you do?"

"We swam . . . and played in the sand," I said as I dried my face.

"Was it big?"

"What?"

"The ship. I heard you went by a ship."

"It was pretty big."

Pyungsoo still had a scar on his face, but he looked healthier than when he first came, and his hair seemed to have grown a lot in the four days we were gone.

"Wait here," I said, and hung the towel on the clothesline and got the shells from my room.

"You found all these on the beach?" he asked excitedly.

I nodded.

"Here, put this one against your ear. You can hear the ocean," I said.

His mouth opened wide. "How does it do that?"

"It lives in the ocean, so it sounds like it."

He looked at the mouth of the shell and put it against his ear again.

"Was the water really salty?" he asked.

"Only if you drank it."

Pyungsoo cocked his head and smiled.

"What did you do?" I asked.

"Nothing. We went to Dr. Pae's. He's going to take the cast off in a couple of weeks." Pyungsoo scuffed the tip of his right sneaker against the cement border of the garden. "We also went to Mrs. Kim's."

"You did?"

He nodded.

"You went to visit her at her house? Just like that, with the cast on?"

He nodded. "Your grandmother said when the cast comes off I'll be visiting Mrs. Kim and Mr. Kim. I may even live there and have my own room."

I looked in the direction of the kitchen but didn't see Mother there.

When we gathered in the living area to eat breakfast, I noticed that Mother's hair was pretty. It looked like Mrs. Park's, high on top and tapered close to her neck in the back. Even the front was nicely brushed to one side, like a wave. When I thought she was in the kitchen, she had gone to a beauty salon.

"You look comfortable in that haircut," Grandmother said while chewing her food.

"I thought it might be easier to take care of," Mother said politely.

"What made you cut your hair?"

"It was . . . very hot there and I thought a change would be good."

Grandmother nodded, observing Mother, then Father, who was stuffing a large piece of *kimchee* into his mouth.

"So you swam?" Grandmother asked us.

"Yes, Grandmother," we answered.

"What else did you do?"

"We played in the sand and ate crabs," Moonhee said.

"Did Father teach you how to swim?"

No one answered.

"No . . . not this time," I finally said.

"Then what did Father do?"

"He made a stew for us," I said.

"Your father made a stew?" Grandmother sounded very surprised. "How did it taste?" she asked, still watching Father.

"Good," I said.

"I've never tasted his stew," Grandmother said with her thin lips stretching over her fake teeth. "I never allow him in the kitchen."

Mother lowered her eyes. I felt bad that I had told Grandmother about our stew, but no one was saying anything.

"Father went deep-sea fishing," I said, trying to distract her from the stew.

"He did? With all of you?" Grandmother asked.

"No . . . he went alone . . ."

"Alone? For a day?"

This time I didn't say anything.

"For two days, yes, alone." Father said, staring at me, annoyed.

Grandmother nodded slowly, as if she understood something. Then she cleared her throat. "I talked to Mrs. Kim about the boy. When she saw him she took a liking to him. It seems like they may want him, even though Mr. Kim needs more persuading. When Pyungsoo's cast comes off we'll visit both of them."

No one said anything and Grandmother went on with what had happened while we were gone, but I could see that neither Mother nor Father was listening.

After Father left for work, Mother went to Grandmother's room and didn't come out for a long time—

longer than she usually spent getting permission for anything. The last time she went behind Grandmother's closed door was for Changhee Uhnni. The parents of the student who received the highest marks at school usually treated all the teachers to a sumptuous meal, and Mother needed money.

The time before that was for herself. She wanted to take a special sewing class to help out her friend Mrs. Park at her boutique, but Grandmother said no to that. Grandmother said she didn't think a good housewife should be working for a clothing boutique, even though Mother said she would be making the clothes at home.

Mother came out from Grandmother's room and went to her vegetable garden, closing the door tightly behind her. She stayed there for a good while, but when she came out her eyes didn't droop and her mouth was not clamped down from anger. She just got very busy unpacking our bags from the trip and instructing Soonja Uhnni to wash the dirty clothes and separate the jars that needed to be cleaned from the ones to be thrown out. Mother moved quickly, cleaning and putting things away, and she even went to the market in the afternoon.

The way Mother went about doing things so efficiently in her new hairdo made her seem like a different person. She moved about with that determined look she had when she stayed up half the night finishing our dresses so we could wear them to church the next morning.

She asked us about our summer projects and reminded us that the recess was more than half over. With Pyungsoo's help I had almost finished my three book reports, but I hadn't started on the insect collection or the art project. I knew I had to catch the insects before the weather turned cooler.

Changhee Uhnni had already finished most of her summer assignments except for the art project, which she was just starting. She drew a design of a matchstick house she was going to build. When she asked Mother how the drawing was, Mother said, "Good," then turned around to do something else, but came back to look at it again and said, "Good," a second time.

The next morning, as soon as Grandmother left to visit a sick friend, Mother put on her makeup and got ready to go out. I hadn't seen her asking Grandmother about an outing so I was surprised when Mother asked us, "Who wants to go to Grandma Min's today?"

Before we could scream, "Me!" Mother said Pyungsoo was going. She only took two at a time because she said four children were too many to take on a bus. Even though going to our maternal grand-mother's house was a treat, Changhee Uhnni glared at Pyungsoo and backed out. Moonhee and Keehee didn't insist when I said I wanted to go. I had a feeling that Mother had planned to take me and Pyungsoo all along.

CHAPTER 22

To Grandma Min's

Our maternal grandmother lived on the other side of the Han River, and the bus ride was long. Mother sat behind us and seemed completely lost in her thoughts. I kept turning around, and finally Mother smiled, gave Pyungsoo and me each a candy, and patted my head.

Pyungsoo and I sucked on our candies and looked out the window. A man pulling a rickshaw full of round watermelons was walking so fast that he looked like he was running. As the bus passed by him, it seemed as if he were going backward. Then we passed a row of small stores with fruit laid out in neat stacks. From one of the stores a woman came out with a large basin and flung the water across the street. A noodle delivery boy on a bicycle, holding a tin box with one hand, cursed at the woman as his bicycle slipped on the wet road. When we neared downtown, there were rows of stores with brightly colored dresses, high-heeled shoes, and shiny furniture.

We got off at the stop near a market and Mother bought some grapes and a watermelon. They looked heavy in her hands as we walked up a hill to Grandma Min's street. Her house was on the left side with gray iron doors.

I called out loudly, "Grandma," and she ran out asking, "Who is it?" even though she knew who it was. When she saw me, she pulled me in with her half-wet hands and hugged me. She smiled at Mother.

"That's the best haircut I've seen on you." Grandma Min always spoke with so much energy—as if everything she said was in a big hurry. "Why, a young person like you shouldn't have to wear a bun in this day and age."

Mother smiled back and handed Grandma the fruits.

"Was the market crowded?"

"No, Mother. You look flushed. What were you doing?"

They always greeted each other by asking questions, but they were really listening to each other's voices and watching their expressions to see if everything was all right.

"And this is?" Grandma asked me, putting her hand on Pyungsoo's head.

I explained who Pyungsoo was and Grandma shook his hand. Then she led us in, past her friendly sunflowers.

Grandma Min's house had a mellow soybean-paste smell, as if a delicious stew were always on the stove.

There, we didn't have to worry about putting our shoes in a perfect row after taking them off. She didn't mind if one shoe was behind another, as they often were when we ran in quickly, shaking the shoes off our feet one at a time.

Inside, all the doors and windows were left wide open, and the cool breeze made the long wooden rosary on the wall sway.

"You want juice? Soda?"

"Anything is fine," Mother answered for us.

"How about some noodles? Are you hungry, June-hee?" Grandma asked.

Though it wasn't lunchtime, I was always hungry at her house, but Mother said, "Not yet, it's too early."

Mother sat with us and let her mother bring in the drinks from the kitchen. Grandma didn't have a helper. She said she was too impatient to watch someone else do things poorly. The only problem was that when she had to go out to Mass each morning or to the market, she had to ask her neighbor to watch the house.

Grandma came in with the drinks. Then she opened a cabinet door, made a rustling noise, and gave Pyungsoo and me each a chocolate bar. She always had goodies stored away and gave them to us right off.

"I figured you went on your vacation. If you were any darker, I wouldn't have recognized you. How was it?" she asked me as she sat next to me.

"Good. We swam a lot," I said, and she smiled. Grandma and I had the same smile, Mother said. We both had slightly buck teeth and a beauty mark above our lip on the right side.

"Why don't you look more rested?" she asked
Mother.

Mother lay down without answering, and Grandma
slid her a pillow. Mother put her head on it and sighed
in comfort.

Grandma turned to Pyungsoo. "So, how did you
hurt your arm? Fighting?" We liked that she asked us
questions instead of asking Mother about us, as other
adults did.

"I fell off a swing."

"Sungjin pushed him off the swing," Mother corrected.

"Is he still the trouble he's always been?"

"Yes," Mother answered, and Grandma shook her
head.

"Well, how are your sisters?" she turned to me.

"Fine," I said.

"How did you all do in school?"

"Good."

"And how are your grandmother and father?"

"They are fine."

"And your grandmother's health?"

"Fine."

"Are you being a good girl to your mother?"

"She is my right hand," Mother said with her eyes
closed.

"That's my girl." Grandma patted my back.

After a short silence she said to Mother, "It's been
a while."

"A long while since I've been here. I know," Mother
answered.

"Yes, long. . . . Is the helper still diligent? She looked like it the other day, serving soybean soup."

"She works hard."

Grandma moved over to Mother and started to massage her legs, and Mother sighed again.

"Hyungsik is in Taekoo this week," Grandma said as she worked on Mother's upper leg. "There is some meeting there at the Seminary. They wanted him to give a lecture." Our priest-uncle was often called to teach or give talks.

"How is he?"

"Busy as usual. I went to his church a few weeks ago. He had two sets of underclothes and one pair of socks in the drawer. I didn't even ask what he did with all the new ones I bought him."

"You shouldn't go there too often. Parishioners will talk."

"What can they say?"

"That you are too indulgent. You shouldn't worry about him. God will take care of him."

"You are right," Grandma sighed. "But couldn't he keep just a few necessary things for himself?"

"Don't worry, Mother," Mother said, and stretched out her hand for Grandma to massage. "How about you children playing outside?" Mother asked us.

Grandma got up and gave me a hat.

"You are already too burnt," she said, and when she saw Pyungsoo eyeing my hat, she gave him one too.

They were waiting for us to move out of earshot. I led Pyungsoo to the vegetable garden. There were peppers, cucumbers, zucchini, green leaf lettuce, and tomatoes. We picked the ripened tomatoes and ate them without even washing them, and went over to the flower garden and sucked on the salvia tubes for their sweet juice. Pyungsoo helped me pick the red, orange, and pink petals of *bongsunwha*, and we put them in my hat. Every summer we dyed our fingernails with the crushed petals from our garden, but ours weren't as colorful. Then I went over to the bright magenta coxcombs and rubbed my cheeks on a velvety flower.

"Put your cheek here—feel it," I said to Pyungsoo.

"You are going to go blind," he said. "You shouldn't rub flowers on your face."

"Why not?"

"If the powder goes in your eyes, you'll go blind."

"Who told you that?" I asked.

"My sister."

"That's silly. It's the powder from the moth's wings that blinds you."

"No, it's true. My older sister said so."

"She did?"

Pyungsoo nodded and said, "You better wash your face."

I got up and walked over to the well.

As I was passing by Grandma Min's room, I heard her say, "You can adopt the boy for the sake of helping him, but if you adopt him for yourself, that's another story."

"What's wrong with having human desire?" Mother asked.

I squatted next to the room and put my ear close to the wall.

"Don't be childish. God did not give you a son."

"He did not give me a male." Mother sounded bitter. "Besides, it's not up to you."

"They say after three children, daughters-in-law are no longer afraid of their mothers-in-law and husbands. I have four—I can say at least one thing I want."

"You did, and your mother-in-law said no."

"She didn't say no. She said she would think about it."

"It's the same. She doesn't want you to bring in an outsider. Didn't your husband say no?"

"He may bend under his mother's thumb."

"That's some way to talk about your children's father."

"If only my mother-in-law would say yes, then. . . . She talks enough about how she is worried about us when we get old. I guess she really means her son." Mother sighed loudly and then there was a silence.

"You are blessed," Grandma said. "You have a home, a husband, food on the table, children in private school. Most people envy your position."

"I guess I'm happy then," Mother said sarcastically.

"Your husband brings home his salary and he doesn't hit you after he drinks."

"Yes, I'm happy."

"Besides, this world is just a test. . . . Life is suffering."

I heard Pyungsoo's footsteps and quickly went over to the well.

Until lunchtime Pyungsoo and I looked for caterpillars in the green leaf lettuce and thought of ways to catch butterflies and dragonflies for my insect collection, but without a net it was very difficult. We tried to trick the dragonflies by circling our fingers while standing behind them to make them dizzy, but that didn't work.

When Grandma called us to lunch we were starving. She made noodles mixed in a hot, peppery sauce, and brought them in with her summer *kimchee* of deep green turnip leaves. Both were so hot they turned my face red.

Mother didn't seem to be in a bad mood because after lunch she spat out her watermelon seeds like a child and laughed at Grandma's stories about her neighbor. Grandma Min said one of her neighbors married this man who she thought was only five years her junior but it turned out they were seven years apart. The neighbor was an instructor who taught how to distinguish male chicks from female chicks. Grandma said she should have known not to marry a man who couldn't tell the difference between male and female.

When we were too full to eat another bite, we lay down and let the fan cool us, and listened to Grandma's voice humming and vibrating.

Mother woke us up and told us it was time to leave. Grandma came out to the bus stop with us.

"Here—here is a little something for you." Grandma handed Mother an envelope. Mother refused it but Grandma put it in Mother's dress pocket. "Get a dress or shoes or something. Go ahead."

When Mother took it out and handed it back, Grandma gently pushed Mother's hand away.

"What money do you have? I should be giving you money, Mother," Mother said regretfully.

"I am all right. You get something." They went

through this every time they met, and Mother ended up taking the money.

"Be thankful for what you have," Grandma said.

Mother looked out the window as the bus pulled away. Grandma waved to us. She looked like she was crying.

CHAPTER 23

To Mrs. Park's

At an unfamiliar stop Mother told us we were getting off. We followed her quickly out of the bus into a fashion district where clothing boutiques lined both sides of the street. Before I could ask where we were going, Mother pushed open a door and I saw Mrs. Park sitting on her couch with a magazine. Then I recognized Mrs. Park's boutique.

"I called you just a few days ago. When did you get back?" Mrs. Park said, approaching us. She had a very pretty face with clear skin and long, dark eyelashes. She was almost beautiful with her mouth closed, but when she smiled, showing her crooked teeth, she looked warm and friendly.

"Yesterday," Mother said.

"And you are out today? Did something happen? Were you thrown out?" Mrs. Park said in her half-joking tone.

Mother just smiled sadly, and Mrs. Park put her hand on Mother's arm, then turned to us.

"Junehee," she said to me, "you've gotten so tall."

"I'm the fifth-tallest girl in my class," I told her.

"I'll bet. Who is this? Your friend?"

I nodded.

Mother explained quickly who Pyungsoo was and how he had hurt his arm. Mrs. Park listened and smiled at Pyungsoo.

"Would you like some cookies?" she asked us when Mother finished explaining.

"They ate a lot already," Mother said.

"Not here they didn't," Mrs. Park said, and called her assistant to bring out some treats.

"How long has he been with you?" Mrs. Park asked Mother.

"About a month."

"We haven't spoken for that long? No, we did but . . . Oh, your mother-in-law was there," she said.

We sat on the couch and ate the cookies her assistant brought out. Mother and Mrs. Park sat on the other couch across from us, turned toward each other. Mother once said if she had a sister she would be like Mrs. Park.

"Your hair—finally, you had the guts to cut it. What did your mother-in-law say?"

"She said it looked cool," Mother said sarcastically.

"At least she doesn't tell you to your face that you can't cut your hair."

"She might as well."

"Your new hair is terrific. It deserves a new dress. What do you think, Junehee? Doesn't Mother need a new dress?" she asked me.

I nodded eagerly. Mrs. Park went to the back room and brought out a bright yellow dress with a green-and-black poppy flower print.

"A customer ordered this but I can make her a new one. She is about your size."

"That's too bright and too short," Mother said, wincing.

"You don't own a dress that is not brown or beige."

"I own bright *hanbok*," Mother said.

"Everybody owns a bright *hanbok*." Mrs. Park handed the dress to Mother and gently pushed her in the direction of the back room where she could change.

When Mother closed the door, Mrs. Park said, "You know that your mother trusts you the most?"

I smiled even though I wasn't sure why adults sometimes said that.

"You had fun at the beach?"

I nodded.

"Who became the darkest?"

"Changhee Uhnni," I answered.

"Did Pyungsoo go with you?"

I shook my head.

Mother came out and she looked big and colorful, wearing the sleeveless above-the-knee dress. Mother didn't own anything that short or without any sleeves.

"You look ten years younger," Mrs. Park said.

Mother looked at herself in the full-length mirror, turning this way and that way. She didn't stand up perfectly straight as Father did in front of a mirror but slouched a little. Mother was taller and bigger than many mothers we knew, and often older relatives commented on how Mother was good daughter-in-law material because she looked strong.

"Where would I wear this to?"

"The same place you wear your new hair."

"She won't like it," Mother said.

"She doesn't like anything, so it doesn't matter. Besides, you look handsome."

At that remark, Mother straightened her back, fixed her new hairdo, and smoothed the front of the dress.

"She'll probably throw me out of the house, you know."

"Good, then you can come live with me," Mrs. Park said confidently.

"And your husband?" Mother had on her clever smile, the corners of her mouth slightly turned down.

"We'll throw him out." Mrs. Park winked at me.

"Two very exemplary wives, aren't we?" Mother said, and they both laughed.

"I can leave early. Let's go over to my house," Mrs. Park suggested.

"I can't. I have to go home. I didn't even tell their grandmother I was going out."

"Then what's the difference if you are late? It only takes ten minutes to go to my house."

"I can't. I have to prepare dinner," Mother said. "I really can't."

"All right then, let me ride with you to your home."

"After I change," Mother said.

"No," Mrs. Park said.

"I can't go home in this dress."

"Why not? You look handsome. Wear your dress—tell your mother-in-law I forced you."

Mother decided to keep the dress on. Outside, her dress looked brighter and bigger. On the way home in Mrs. Park's car, Mother began telling her all about Pyungsoo.

Pyungsoo had already fallen asleep leaning on my shoulder, and soon my eyes grew heavy too.

A bump on the road woke me up.

"When I become a mother-in-law, I'm not going to live with my son. They can live where they want to," Mrs. Park said.

"The very few who say that become the most difficult mothers-in-law."

"You really think I'll be like that?" Mrs. Park asked.

"Worse."

They laughed.

"What are you going to do?" Mrs. Park asked.

"Do I have any choice?"

"Maybe."

"Maybe . . ." Mother repeated slowly.

"It's going to be very difficult," Mrs. Park said. "Even if you can keep the boy."

"I know that already."

They paused.

"How's Changhee's Father? Handsome as ever?"

"Too handsome," Mother answered.

"Does he still come home late?" Mrs. Park asked carefully.

"Mostly."

"They do return, you know. When they see no one is as faithful as their wives." When Mother didn't say anything, Mrs. Park added, "Sometimes I can't believe I married a man almost fifteen years older, but I'm glad that he has gotten his womanizing out of his system. They all go through that stage, you know that," she said.

"Meanwhile?"

"You wait. They'll soon be tired of drinking and listening to cheap women. You just say to yourself, I don't need any of this."

I had my eyes closed but some gesture of Mrs. Park's made Mother laugh out loud.

At first Grandmother didn't say anything to Mother when she saw the bright green dress. She just nodded and gave her a wry smile. Mother explained that we went to Grandma Min's house and stopped by Mrs. Park's on the way back. Grandmother waited for Mother to explain why. When she didn't offer any excuse, Grandmother looked at Mother's dress more closely, as if that could explain something.

"Where did you get that dress?"

"Jongmee gave it to me."

"Is that the style now?" Grandmother asked, taking off her reading glasses.

"I don't know, Mother. She knows about these things," Mother said politely.

"I see." Grandmother nodded. "Maybe they are meant to be worn by younger women."

Mother didn't reply "yes" as she usually did but just went to her room to change into work clothes.

I went to my room with Pyungsoo. I had instructed him to offer Changhee Uhnni the chocolate I saved from Grandma Min's. She was building the match house for her summer project.

"Here." Pyungsoo handed her the chocolate bar. Changhee Uhnni looked at him, then me, and turned away.

"It's for you." Pyungsoo offered one more time when I nodded to him. Changhee Uhnni snatched it out of Pyungsoo's hand and put it next to the match house.

"Grandma Min said to say hello," I said, but she didn't say anything. "I brought back *bongsunwha* petals. We could dye our nails tonight."

Changhee Uhnni looked up. "Let me see."

I showed her a paper bag full of petals.

"I'm first," she said, and I nodded. She always got to do everything first anyway.

That evening Soonja Uhnni crushed the flower petals with alum powder. She put wet little clumps on Changhee Uhnni's fingernails and wrapped them with leaves, and then with a piece of plastic to make sure they didn't leak overnight. I was next, then Moonhee and Keehee. When we were finished, we went to sleep with our hands sticking outside the blanket. Changhee Uhnni complained that her fingers were itchy and uncomfortable, but finally she fell asleep and the room became quiet.

In the dark I thought about the word Mrs. Park said that afternoon, "womanizing." Father was womanizing with bar girls. I smelled my fingers with their crushed flower petals and wondered if those women smelled like flowers. Then I put my mouth on the back of my hand and bit it as hard as I could.

CHAPTER 24

To Great-Aunt's

I was relieved when Grandmother didn't ask anything about our trip to Grandma Min's the following day, but I avoided her anyway. Grandmother was unusually quiet. She took out her Bible and read it for a long time, often taking off her reading glasses and cleaning them slowly, and then opened the hymn book and sang her favorite: "We do not know what will happen tomorrow, we don't even know what will happen today, but God knows. . . ."

At meals she watched Mother carefully and Mother, knowing she was doing so, became silent.

During breakfast Grandmother cleared her throat.

"I thought I'd visit your aunt today."

"What for?" Father asked.

Grandmother didn't go to her older sister's unless there was some kind of event like a wedding, a funeral, or a family crisis. Our great-aunt was the oldest and wealthiest relative she had and the person whose opinion Grandmother respected most.

"Well, I haven't seen her since January . . . and her birthday is coming up."

"Why don't you take the boy with you and see if she'll take him?" Father asked.

"She has enough people depending on her." Grandmother cleared her throat again. "We are well off enough to take care of our own problems."

"When are you going to bring him to the Kims again?" Father asked.

"I told you, when the cast comes off. Mr. Kim needs to see the boy at his best."

"That's not for a while, and even then, we don't know if they'll take him," Father said in his argumentative tone.

"Let's see what happens," Grandmother said.

"She can definitely afford it."

"We'll see."

Mother picked up the empty bowls and left the room. Father watched Grandmother staring at Mother's back.

"Did their mother say anything to you?" he asked.

"Well . . . we did have a talk."

"What about?"

"We'll discuss that when I come back. Let's not talk now in front of the children."

Father just shook his head. "I told her no."

"Let me handle this."

"There is nothing to handle," Father said, gritting his teeth.

"I worry, though," Grandmother said carefully.

"When you get old . . . You are still young, so you wouldn't be thinking about that now, but . . ."

Father glared at Grandmother. "I told you—"

"I know what you told me," Grandmother said angrily. "Mothers worry about their sons."

Father didn't say any more after that.

I didn't have to sleep with Mother and Father to know that Father wasn't speaking to her even when they were in their room. Since returning from vacation, Mother stayed up late before going to her room. Laying in my room I counted the times her long shadow moved across our rice-paper door before I fell asleep.

Grandmother put on her best jade-colored *hanbok* and carefully spread lipstick on her made-up face. Mother combed Pyungsoo's hair and put on his blue shirt-and-pants set as Grandmother instructed. Pyungsoo looked at me when no one was watching and mouthed for me to come with him.

"Grandmother, can I come with you?" I asked.

She looked at me and hesitated. "I guess you can come with me."

"Me too, me too," Moonhee said when she heard me ask.

When our taxi had left our neighborhood, Grandmother turned to me.

"How was your maternal grandmother?"

"Fine," I answered.

"What did she say about Pyungsoo?"

"Nothing."

"Did your mother say anything about him?"

"We played outside."

"Did you stay there long?"

"We had lunch there."

"Then you went to see Mrs. Park?"

"Yes, Grandmother."

"Did she pick out that dress for Mother?"

"Yes."

"What did she say about Pyungsoo?"

"She just asked who he was."

"And?"

"Mother told her he was Grandmother Boksoon's grandson."

"And?"

"That's all," I said.

Grandmother sighed and stopped asking me questions.

When the taxi honked at the gate of our great-aunt's mansion, the gatekeeper came out and, recognizing Grandmother, bowed deeply. We drove up the pebbled road, which was lined with mossy rocks and cone-shaped evergreens, and came to a large ground. On the right side was a fenced area for the two German shepherds and two *jindos* that barked incessantly at the guests, and on the left was a big garden full of different-colored roses, geraniums, rose moss, salvias, canna, begonias, and pine trees. Everything in Great-Aunt's place was perfectly arranged. In the back of the mansion was a mountain they owned themselves. When the weather was nice Great-Aunt let us walk around in it accompanied by one of her gardeners.

The taxi drove up to the house and servants ran out and helped Grandmother out of the car. Great-Aunt trailed after them, and behind her were two of her four daughters-in-law. Great-Aunt had four sons and a daughter, but only the two oldest sons and their families lived with her. Her first daughter-in-law, with a white and prosperous moon face, smiled at Grandmother after bowing, and the second daughter-in-law, with a pale, egg-shaped face, stood behind her and hardly smiled.

"Why didn't you call me? I could have sent you a car." Great-Aunt always spoke with vigor.

Great-Aunt had Grandmother's face but her features were not as small and delicate. She had bigger eyes and longer teeth and a heavier northern accent, and Grandmother spoke more like her when she was there.

"That's why I didn't call you. I didn't want to bother you."

"Don't be ridiculous," Great-Aunt said.

Even though they were sisters, they went through the whole greeting etiquette as though they were strangers. Grandmother handed her a box of Japanese bean cakes we had picked up on the way. Both sisters loved those sweet bean cakes.

"You didn't have to do this," Great-Aunt said.

"It's nothing." Grandmother's face turned yellow when she was ashamed.

When Great-Aunt visited us, she brought a whole side of beef ribs or a box of exotic sesame-seed candies in an elegant container. Sometimes she even brought foreign fruits like bananas or pineapples.

Moonhee and I bowed deeply, and Pyungsoo bowed after us.

Great-Aunt took Grandmother by her hand and they started to walk toward the house. The daughters-in-law followed them and behind them, us.

The servants put out the slippers for us and then

scurried back to the kitchen to prepare refreshments. In the guest-receiving room were big red lacquered cabinets with ornate designs of hawks and trees in mother-of-pearl, and a round matching table. We sat on an embroidered cushion in red and jade and Great-Aunt sat across from us, next to Grandmother. The two aunts stood by the door.

"Go ahead, sit down," Grandmother said, and they sat.

"It's been too long. Where does the time go?" Great-Aunt said.

"You have gained weight. You look well," Grandmother said, paying Great-Aunt a compliment.

"What weight? I'm still all bones. You need to put on some weight. You are skinnier than I am." That was true. Even though Great-Aunt was thin, she had thicker bones.

"You are well?" Grandmother asked the older daughter-in-law, who smiled and nodded. "How are the children?"

"Studying hard."

"Almost ready for marriage, aren't they?"

"Yes," she said politely.

Grandmother said to the second daughter-in-law, "You need to eat more."

The skinny aunt just lowered her head with her hands gathered in the front.

The servants came bringing ginseng tea with delicate pine nuts floating on top, and soda and cakes for us. They set the refreshments on the round table before us.

"Let's pray first," Great-Aunt said, and I knew the tea would get cold before the prayer was over. Grandmother and Great-Aunt, both Methodists, said long prayers.

We closed our eyes and Great-Aunt started the prayer by asking for forgiveness and blessings for our family. Then Grandmother continued with asking the same for Great-Aunt, her dead husband, her five children, their wives, and their children, naming each one of them, and then more relatives, their families, local and national politicians, President Park Chunghee, and even Kim Il Sung, the president of North Korea. Finally, she asked for guidance on the fate of Pyungsoo.

We reached for our cakes when they said to go ahead and eat.

"Your mother pregnant yet?" Great-Aunt always asked that question whenever she saw us. We shook our heads. "Tell her to get pregnant. She needs a son." Great-Aunt turned to Grandmother. "Chungsik's wife is pregnant with the fifth one." Chungsik was her third son, who also had four daughters. "They are hopeful. Usually the fifth one is a boy."

"That's . . . I don't know. You know the Nhos. They kept making her daughter-in-law try. She has six grand-daughters now," Grandmother said.

"So? Try it again."

"Is it that easy?" Grandmother lowered her voice. "Changhee's Mother has weak ovaries. You remember the two premature babies."

"Give her some Chinese medicine."

"I did. Anyway, their father feels . . ."

"Try again, I tell you," Great-Aunt said impatiently.

Grandmother shook her head slowly, then her eyes fell on Pyungsoo. Great-Aunt also looked at him.

"He is a small one. How old is he? Who is he?"

Grandmother told how Pyungsoo came to be in our house and how he broke his arm. When she was finished the daughters-in-law clucked their tongues and looked at him with sympathetic eyes.

"I'll see what I can do," Great-Aunt said. "He may be able to stay with one of the gardeners."

"No," Grandmother said hesitantly. "I don't mean that he needs a home. I mean, he does, but that's not why . . ."

Great-Aunt waited for Grandmother to explain.

"I'm worried about Jungmin. What is he going to do when he gets old? Who is going to take care of him?"

"Send your daughter-in-law to a Chinese—"

Grandmother interrupted, "*Ahigo*, she is already thirty-eight. Besides, their father doesn't want to try anymore."

"He will be happy when he gets a son."

"So . . . I thought maybe the boy . . ." Grandmother trailed off.

Great-Aunt knitted her eyebrows. "He wants to adopt the boy?"

"No, he doesn't. . . . I just thought. . . . I am worried about him. I could die more peacefully if I knew he too had someone to look after him."

"That's nonsense! Adopting a boy out of your blood-line? He could live with you as a kind of houseboy, but have him as a grandson? Adopted children don't take care of their parents. They rebel when they grow up. It's not a good idea."

Pyungsoo stopped eating. Grandmother sighed loudly.

"Tell Changhee's Mother to use our Chinese medicine doctor," Great-Aunt said again. Then she asked her second daughter-in-law to go get some more tea. When the skinny aunt left, Great-Aunt leaned over to Grandmother and quietly asked, "Jungmin doesn't have a son anywhere?"

Grandmother's face turned white. "What kind of talk is that?"

"Doesn't he have a woman somewhere?"

"How could he have a woman on his salary? Only the rich—like your sons—have women and second homes. Let's not talk about this in front of the children."

Great-Aunt glanced over at us. "What do they know? Kwangsik has a second family with two sons." He was the second son, whose wife was the skinny aunt.

Grandmother said determinedly, "Jungmin has no second home."

"Even if he doesn't have a home, he may have a son. Do you remember all those women who used to follow him around?"

Great-Aunt persisted, smiling as though it were amusing, but Grandmother put up her hand in protest. Besides, we heard the slippers of the second aunt.

When she came into the room, Great-Aunt told her to get the gardener. She came back with the gruff man who seemed happy to show us the peacocks in front of Great-Aunt. But as soon as we were outside, he put a cigarette in his mouth and told us to follow him.

"What is 'premature,' and what woman does Father have?" Moonhee asked me quietly.

"I don't know," I lied.

In the fenced area behind the mansion, peacocks with

open tails strutted around the cage, and the green eyes on their feathers watched us. The gardener explained that the ones with the beautiful tails were male and the brown ones running away from them were female.

We circled the house and walked up a trail in the mountain. When we came back down to the large ground, we visited the dogs, who snarled at us and showed their teeth.

"See? That's a bitch." The gardener pointed to the white one. "She's ferocious," he said with a smirk to Pyungsoo.

We were glad when the servant came out and called us in for lunch.

A large table was set up in the guest-receiving room. On the table were three different kinds of *kimchee*—cucumber, green leaf, and one in cold soup; a stack of mung-bean pancakes with delicate designs made of slivered red peppers; a cold sesame soup with quail eggs; vermicelli noodles mixed with colorful vegetables; sliced pressed meat; and roasted fish. It looked like someone's birthday table.

"Let's eat." Great-Aunt picked up her spoon after the prayer and we started. Even with his awkward left hand, Pyungsoo ate everything and asked for a second bowl of rice, but Moonhee picked at her food in her usual way. I ate a lot of the pressed meat even though I wasn't very hungry.

Great-Aunt put a piece of fish on Grandmother's bowl and said, "Here, have one more." But Grandmother put it back on Great-Aunt's bowl, saying that she had had enough. Great-Aunt then put a piece of meat on Grandmother's rice bowl, and they kept doing this throughout lunch.

After the meal the table was cleared and fruits were brought in, but Grandmother didn't eat, saying that she had a headache. Great-Aunt arranged for her son to send his car.

When it was time to leave, Great-Aunt gave each of us a thousand won, despite Grandmother's protest. Only on January first did we get such a large sum, when we did our traditional bowing for the new year to all of our relatives. As we were leaving, Great-Aunt said she would tell the Chinese medicine doctor to expect Mother, but Grandmother shook her hand.

On the way home, Grandmother put her head back on the seat and didn't say anything. A man ran out from a side street and got almost run over by our car. He screamed, "You think if you own a car, you can kill people with it?" and spat at the car. The driver stopped to get out, but Grandmother said to ignore him, since he was so poor he didn't know what he was saying. So he kept on driving, and soon both Moonhee and Pyungsoo fell asleep on my shoulders. I looked out the window and saw people frowning from the red dust rising as our car passed.

Grandmother said she had a headache from indigestion and went directly to her room to lie down. By dinnertime the three of us were still too full to eat and Grandmother hadn't woken up from her nap. Mother, Changhee Uhnni, Keehee, and the helper ate in the pantry/dining room. I sat with them.

"What time does Father finish at work?" I asked.

"What?" Mother was preoccupied.

"When does Father finish his work?"

"Around six or seven."

"Where does Father go every night until so late?"

"He spends time with friends."

"Which friends?"

"I don't know." Mother looked up at me curiously.

"You don't know them?"

"I know some of them," Mother said.

"Where does Father go out with his friends?"

Mother put down her chopsticks.

"Can't you tell him to come home early?" I asked.

"He does what he pleases." Mother sighed, then asked, "Did Grandmother ask about Pyungsoo?"

I nodded.

"Great Aunt said no?"

I nodded.

CHAPTER 25

The Match House

Evenings were still light until late even though there was a hint of autumn in the cool breeze. After dinner Mother went to her vegetable garden, but she wasn't tending the vegetables when I entered. She was looking out toward the mountain where the leaves had turned to their deepest green before the change.

"Mother," I called, but she didn't answer me right away. "Mother, should I get chopsticks?" We often helped her by picking the caterpillars off the lettuce leaves.

"There are no more caterpillars. They are all gone," Mother answered without turning around.

A red-tailed dragonfly flew around Mother's hair, then out into the pink strip of clouds above the mountain. I remembered how at the beginning of the summer, before *changma*, I saw her standing in the dark with lightning bugs all around.

"Are you going to make our uniforms?"

"Uniforms? Yes, I'll have to get the fabric soon." She paused. "Have you started your insect collection?"

"Not yet."

"Better work on that—not too many days left to summer." Mother was still staring out into the mountains.

We stood silently. When she spoke again she sounded very sad.

"When I was young, maybe six, my father showed me how to dance Western style. He put my feet on top of his and twirled around. No one knew how to dance like that then. We had the only phonograph in our neighborhood and everyone watched us. Then he went to China."

"What was Grandfather doing in China?"

"He went to do some business that didn't work out."

"For how long?"

"Five years," Mother said.

"For so long?"

"In those days they went away for a long time. There were only trains to travel by. I was already in school in Seoul when he returned. Then he was killed."

I had heard about our maternal grandfather's death. During the war, he led an independent civilian group against the North Koreans, and his brother, a general in the army, sent Military Police to protect him. In the middle of the night, Grandfather and the MPs ran into what they thought was a South Korean tank. When a soldier asked for the password, our Grandfather gave them a number. Mother said she would never forget the South Korean password for that night, which got her father killed by the enemy. It was "thirty-three."

"He never saw your father," Mother said. "I wonder . . ."

Soonja Uhnni ran across the yard and opened the door, which was usually barred after dinner, and we heard Father's clicking shoes. Mother and I went out to the courtyard. Father had gone in and Grandmother was instructing Soonja Uhnni to bring in her dinner with Father's. I was starting to get a little hungry.

In the living area Grandmother, Father, and I ate quietly. Mother sat next to us, peeling the skin off the peaches and cutting them for dessert.

"Your aunt is well," Grandmother said deliberately.

Father fidgeted with his chopsticks to separate the roasted dried anchovies.

"She asks every time if Changhee's Mother is pregnant. She said she knows a good Chinese medicine doctor for her."

Father didn't say anything and Grandmother went on as though she didn't notice the muscles on Father's face flexing. "Their third son's wife is pregnant with a fifth child. She said the fifth is usually a boy." Father slowly shook his head in disgust. "She said Changhee's Mother should try one more time," Grandmother persisted.

"How many times do I have to tell you?" Father raised his voice.

"Of course I told her that would be difficult," Grandmother continued as if she didn't hear him. "Your aunt said adopting out of the family line is not acceptable.

She seemed willing to take care of Pyungsoo if the Kims don't want him."

Father didn't say anything after that. Grandmother had said all she wanted to say.

Mother put down the knife and said slowly, "I would like to keep the boy."

Grandmother stopped chewing and Father's eyebrows went all the way up.

"What is it you said, Changhee's Mother?" Grandmother asked, her thin eyelids fluttering.

"I would like to adopt the boy," Mother said without changing her tone.

"Nachom." Father wagged his finger at her. "Don't be ridiculous." He spat out those words and went back to eating noisily.

"Mother, you often said you were worried about your son's future. Wouldn't this be a solution to that?"

"Well . . . I don't know. I don't think it's my decision," Grandmother stammered.

"Then in whose hands does our future lie?" Mother looked Grandmother directly in the eyes.

"My sister said—" Grandmother started.

"She won't be around when your son is as old as she is now. Besides, we didn't look for the boy, he came to us."

"Well . . ."

"Forget about it," Father said, gritting his teeth. "Can't you just forget it?"

"Mother?" Our mother ignored Father and spoke to Grandmother. "Won't you think about your son's future?"

"Don't involve me," Father shouted. "I don't need anyone." Then he got up and left the table.

"I have never gone against my sister. . . . I'll think about it once more," Grandmother said without conviction, then added, "It's better not to expect anything, Changhee's Mother."

Later as I lay in my room, I thought about how Mother looked big and soft as she walked away with the dinner dishes on a tray. I tossed and turned, then started to count the sticks of the match house Changhee Uhnni had built. It was on top of the table where a strip of light coming through the cracks of the sliding doors lit the insides. I wanted to crawl in there and sleep. I would arrange it exactly as I wanted and allow no one in my house. As if she heard my plans, Changhee Uhnni turned over and groaned in her sleep.

Our sliding door opened quietly, and the light from outside poured in and then disappeared as the door closed. First I thought it was Soonja Uhnni bringing water for us, but by the way the large body moved heavily I knew it was Mother. I wanted to call her, but I didn't want her to know I was awake if she wanted to be alone.

Mother faced the wall where the wooden cross hung and took out her rosary. By the little clinking sound I knew it was the clear blue beaded one. I listened to Mother uttering softly the words of the Apostle's Creed, which sounded as familiar as a bedtime story, but in the middle, when Jesus descended, she stopped. Then I heard a thumping noise. The hand holding the rosary was hitting Mother's chest hard.

"Mother," I called out quietly.

She stopped and breathed deeply to calm herself. But I could hear the strain in her voice when she said, "Did I wake you?"

"Mother, why don't you lie down and sleep next to me?" I said.

"No, not now. Go back to sleep. I have to finish my prayer first. Let's not wake Changhee too," she whispered.

We were silent for a while, but I could tell she was not praying.

"I'm sorry I wasn't a boy, Mother," I said.

Mother put her hands on her face and started to cry, almost without a sound—but I could see her shoulders shaking.

Changhee Uhnni stirred, and Mother tried to stop crying and wiped her eyes and nose with her apron. I reached out and touched her arm, which was soft and moist from the tears. She put her hand on my head and whispered, "You are like my son, you are better than a son."

When Mother lay next to me, I tried to give her some of my blanket but she refused. She just lay her hand over her eyes and sighed several times. "Go to sleep," she said, but for a long time I just listened to her breathing, waiting for her to fall asleep first. If I were in Changhee Uhnni's match house, I thought, I would allow Mother to live with me.

.   .   .

In the morning I heard Mother's voice and sat up thinking she was next to me, but her voice came from behind our room by the backyard. I cracked the back sliding door and peered out, and there was Mother saying something to Pyungsoo while hugging him.

CHAPTER 26

To Grandfather's

Auntie Yunekyung called, and soon Mother had all of us in our best clothes, except for Pyungsoo and Keehee. Mother said Keehee was too young to visit a sick person. She wasn't even sure if Moonhee was old enough but Moonhee insisted she would be all right. Still, no one told us where we were going and who the sick person was, and every time we asked, Mother said Auntie would explain it to us on our way. Grandmother kept shaking her head, saying, "I don't know, I don't know about this."

Auntie came in her modest red dress. Grandmother said to her that this might not be a good idea, but Auntie piled us in a taxi anyway and we were on our way to a mysterious place.

"Listen carefully," Auntie said. "We are going to visit your grandfather."

"Grandfather?" we asked in unison. "Whose grandfather?"

"Yours—your father's father, my father."

"He is alive?" I asked in disbelief.

We always thought he was dead because when we asked about him, everyone shushed us.

"No, he is very sick, and he wants to see you."

"He is really Father's father?" I asked.

"Yes."

"He was alive all this time?"

"Yes."

"Where does he live?" Moonhee asked.

"In Ewha-dong."

"He lived there all this time?" Moonhee looked very confused.

"Yes, I guess," Auntie said, fixing her hair.

"Does Father know about him?" Changhee Uhnni asked.

"Of course."

"Why didn't anyone tell us?" Changhee Uhnni was getting upset.

"Well . . ." Auntie began but didn't say any more.

All we ever heard about Grandfather was how he had left Grandmother when she was young, and how Grandmother had to live with her in-laws for many years.

The taxi stopped in front of a small house. After Auntie checked to see how we looked, she brushed her fingers on her tongue and fixed Changhee Uhnni's bangs. Then she smoothed my hair, which was pulled back on top with a ribbon. At last she rang the bell.

An old woman opened the door and Auntie greeted her as though she knew her.

"I brought the grandchildren," Auntie said, and the old woman nodded.

We bowed politely and followed Auntie into the house. We sat in their living area with our legs folded under us and our hands on our laps. The living area was as small as our grandmother's room.

When the woman went away, Auntie said, "Call him Grandfather and be very respectful."

The old woman returned with a tray of cookies and drinks and set it in front of us, but none of us touched it.

"Does Father know we are here?" Auntie asked.

"I better go see." She disappeared to one of the rooms and we heard a murmur of voices.

"Should we go over there?" Auntie asked out loud, but no answer came back from the room.

The wooden doors slid open wide, and we saw an old man who could barely walk coming toward us, leaning on the woman. He had dark skin and a few white hairs. We all stood up and bowed.

"Father, hang on to my arm." Auntie helped him down onto the floor.

When Grandfather sat, the old woman went away.

He motioned to us and we sat in front of him. Even though he had only a few white hairs, a sagging chin, and many wrinkles on his forehead, he looked very familiar. He had our father's eyes and forehead. We tried not to stare at him.

Auntie waited for Grandfather to speak first. He pointed at us.

"Yes, Father," Auntie said. "This is the first, Changhee,

second, Junehee, and third, Moonhee. The last one was too young to bring here."

Grandfather nodded, but his head shook sideways at the same time, so it was hard to know whether he understood.

"How are you feeling?" Auntie asked.

"Not too good," he said in a hoarse voice. With his shaking finger he pointed to Changhee Uhnni. "She . . . she looks like her father when he was a boy." He opened his mouth to say something else but closed it.

Changhee Uhnni didn't take her eyes off the old man.

"He is well?" Grandfather asked.

"Yes," Auntie answered.

"I wasn't a good father. . . . You heard?" he said to us.

"Father," Auntie said, "don't say such a thing."

"It's true."

"He is well?" he asked again.

"Yes."

Grandfather closed his eyes. "Do you remember"— he opened his eyes and looked at Auntie—"when he took my fishing rods?" Auntie nodded, but it didn't seem like she did.

Grandfather continued, "Two of them, your father . . ." This time he looked at us. "He was five years old. He was very smart—very. He stacked the bricks and took them down. But he forgot he wasn't supposed to and boasted." Grandfather looked somewhere behind us.

There was a long silence. Auntie, who always filled silence with her birdlike chatter, was quiet.

"I"—Grandfather's eyes welled up as he tried to

speak again—"I . . . don't know what he looks like now." He blinked and tears dropped onto his arm, but he didn't seem to notice them. Auntie took our her perfumed handkerchief and wiped his tears and his nose.

"Are you taking your medicine regularly?" Auntie asked, and Grandfather nodded.

"It's no use, the medicine, doctors, nothing, nothing works now. . . . Your boys, are they—?"

"Yes, they are fine," Auntie answered.

No one said anything and we stared at the floor.

Finally Grandfather said, "I'm tired."

Auntie got up and helped him up. We also got up.

He turned to go, then turned back to us. "I don't want to touch you," he said, withdrawing his shaking hand. "I don't want to contaminate you. I'm very sick." Then he let Auntie take him to his room.

On the way home, Auntie did not stop talking. "Remember, your grandfather comes from a very prominent family in Pyongyang. Before the war broke out, his house had twenty-five rooms and so many servants that your grandmother thought she was in a palace. The storage room was filled with high stacks of rice, I remember that. Then the war broke out and we had to flee to the south. They lost everything."

Auntie often talked about our family as if we came from royalty. She explained that the old woman was his second wife and they had a son we never saw.

When we were almost home, Moonhee, who was holding my hand, threw up into the handkerchief and cried. Auntie had to carry her up the stairs, and seeing her so pale, Mother regretted sending her for the visit.

Moonhee kept saying, "His tears dropped from the tip of his nose," and Mother had to hold her and rock her until she fell asleep.

Even though Auntie told us not to tell Father about the trip, Grandmother mentioned it that night.

"Your sister took the children to see your father."

"What?"

"He is dying." Grandmother offered an explanation.

"Nachom." Father looked away. "I don't care if he is already dead. I told you never to mention him around me and you let her take them?"

"He is dying. After all, he was your father."

"So?"

"He wanted to see them. How could I refuse?"

"How could you let her take them?" Father said.

"It was a long time ago," Grandmother said. "It doesn't matter now."

"How could you? Why did you let her take the children?" Father shouted.

"Don't shout at me."

"Why did you let her take the children?"

"Stop shouting!" Grandmother shouted back.

Father went into his room and came back dressed to go out.

"Where are you going?"

Father didn't answer but put on his shoes and left.

"Didn't Grandfather look just like Father?" I asked Changhee Uhnni at night when we were ready to sleep.

"No, nothing like Father."

"You didn't think he looked like Father?"

"No," she said. "I hope I never see him again." She turned away.

I couldn't get the picture of Grandfather out of my mind—his bent fingers, the wrinkles, his head shaking all the time, and the sickeningly sweet smell that stayed with me like the smell of a hospital. The old woman, his second wife, looked older than our grandmother, and she had on a worn gray skirt and yellow-white blouse, things our grandmother would never wear around guests. She really didn't look like she could have been a bar girl who poured drinks.

CHAPTER 27

The Net

For a couple of days, no one seemed to be concerned about Pyungsoo. Father called Auntie Yunekyung and fought with her, and she yelled at Grandmother for telling him. No one knew that Grandfather had died three days after we saw him because Auntie didn't tell us. Finally when she let Mother know, Mother told Grandmother and Father. Father didn't stop reading the paper, but his knuckles turned white.

I tried to keep Pyungsoo out of everybody's way and didn't ask when his cast was coming off or anything else, in order not to remind Grandmother about him. Mother too kept him out of Grandmother's and Father's way. She served them their meals first and brought us ours later, and only after Father left for work did she wash Pyungsoo's face and change his clothes.

We had just over a week left to our summer recess, and the only project I was finished with was the book reports. The insect collection was the most difficult one, and I had only gathered a few common ones like the cabbage butterflies and dragonflies from our yard. They barely filled a third of the wooden box I had bought for the collection.

"I can help you catch them," Pyungsoo offered when he saw me rearranging the insects.

"You have a broken arm," I said.

"Look, it's almost better." He wiggled his fingers protruding from the cast and smiled. "Besides, I can catch with one arm."

Pyungsoo and I went to the storage room to look for the green insect net, but we found out that while we were away, Sungjin had borrowed it and had broken the strings. The one good thing that came out of Pyungsoo's broken arm was that this was the only time our cousin came over to the house the entire month.

I went around the rice sacks toward the back of the storage room to find the nylon string I could use to patch the net. In a dark corner I felt something running over my foot and shrieked. A mouse scurried away and Pyungsoo chased after it. Then he came back, took my hand, and led me out of the storage room. His hand was cool and bony, not clammy like my partner's at school.

Mother washed my foot, put Mercurochrome on the invisible scratches, and gave me some money for a new net. Then she rummaged through her purse again and took out two more ten-won notes.

"Here," she gave them to Pyungsoo. "Buy something you like."

"Thank you." He held the bills in his hand. Then in a tiny voice he said, "Mother."

Mother looked at him wistfully, then closed her purse with a click and turned away. Pyungsoo folded the bills carefully and put them in his pocket.

As we walked down our street, Pyungsoo held my hand and then let it go when we got to the main street. Instead, he carried the jar I was holding for the insects.

"You stay here, I'll go get it," I said when we reached Mr. Moon's shop, but he followed me into the store, saying under his breath, "I'm not afraid of him."

Mr. Moon, who was reading the paper, looked up at us with his glasses hanging from his nose.

"He's still with you, is he?" he asked in his nasal voice.

"Yes. We need a net to catch insects." I took out the money to assure Mr. Moon.

He pointed at the stack without taking his eyes off Pyungsoo. "Go bring me one."

Pyungsoo stood by the door and pretended he didn't notice Mr. Moon's stare. He studied the holes in the lid of the glass jar.

I took a green net out of the stack and handed the money to Mr. Moon. He whispered to me, although the store was so small that there was no point in whispering.

"Tell your mother to come down here and leave me some advance if she wants that orphan to come into my store. Otherwise he should be accompanied by an adult."

I said loudly, "He is not an orphan anymore."

"Heh?"

"Grandmother decided to adopt him. He is my brother now." I lied without blinking an eye.

"Brother?" He glanced at Pyungsoo.

"Yes." I had lied before, but I hardly ever lied to an adult I wasn't related to.

"Then don't say anything to your mother." Mr. Moon's tone changed. "Will he be going to your school?"

I nodded.

"Well then, he'll be needing new school supplies."

Mr. Moon came out from behind the counter with a box that he had stashed away for the occasions when parents came with children. He took out two small boxes of caramels and handed one to me and the other to Pyungsoo. He refused.

"You don't have to pay. It's a gift for you," Mr. Moon said.

I took the boxes, thanked him for both of us, and then left. When we were in the street, Mr. Moon rushed out with the net. Caught up in my lie, I had left it behind. I thanked him again and he smiled, showing his yellow teeth. "Tell your mother school starts soon."

"Why did you say that?" Pyungsoo asked as we headed toward the mountain.

"Mr. Moon will treat you better that way."

Pyungsoo was kicking small pebbles as we walked.

"Mrs. Kim said I could have my own room."

"So?"

"So, you don't have to lie."

"I wasn't lying. Mother wanted to adopt you, stupid!"

The rest of the way we walked up in silence. I tried to walk ahead of him, but by the time we reached the mountain I wasn't so angry anymore. I really shouldn't have lied.

We squatted in the grass and waited for insects to appear. Pyungsoo put his good arm around my shoulders and whispered, "See that?" We saw a butterfly fluttering around a yellow flower and waited for it to land. I got up slowly with the net and tiptoed toward it, but the orange butterfly got away. Then I chased after a grasshopper and caught it, and put it in the jar. Pyungsoo wanted to try the net too, but I was afraid he would trip. So he stood in the grass and pointed whenever he saw one leaping in the air. We finally caught another grasshopper and found a dead cicada under a tree.

As we walked home he said, "See? I told you I could help. I'll help you catch some more."

I smiled at him and he squeezed my hand.

Near home, with the money Mother gave him, he bought two fruit ice bars and gave one to me. I held the jar so he could eat with his good hand.

PART IV

The
Son

CHAPTER 28

 The Lie

I was just about to ask Mother if Pyungsoo and I could walk up to the mountains to collect some more insects when Grandmother announced this was the day Pyungsoo's cast was coming off. She was going to take him to Dr. Pae's herself. I volunteered to go along and she agreed reluctantly.

Grandmother was strangely particular about what Pyungsoo should wear to see Dr. Pae, and even made me change to my dressy clothes. Grandmother had on a nice pale yellow *hanbok* with a brown topaz broach.

The day was cool, and on the way to Dr. Pae's office I saw a neat stack of round golden pears at the general store. They would not be as sweet and juicy as the ones sold in the middle of September, but they were a definite sign of autumn.

Grandmother was unusually quiet, and she kept adjusting her fake bun, which was slightly lopsided. We walked behind her and Pyungsoo tried to hold my hand, but I pulled it away and shook my head.

"How is his arm going to look?" I asked Grandmother, but she didn't answer.

"It's going to look strange," Pyungsoo said as we walked up the staircase to Dr. Pae's office. "I can't wait to scratch it."

I waited in the outer office while Grandmother and Pyungsoo went into the examination room. No one else was there, so I walked around looking at the photograph of President Park Chunghee on the wall and a calendar with a Buddha picture. On the small table was a brass ashtray with a painting of an old king's palace, Kyungbok-koong, which we had visited on a school trip.

Even if Pyungsoo had to live with the Kims, he would be in my grade, I told myself, maybe even in my class. If not, I would see him at lunchtime or after school. Before school Moonhee and I walked together with Changhee Uhnni, who didn't let us stop to talk with our friends. But after school we were on our own.

I hadn't seen Grandmother make any calls to the Kims, and she hadn't spoken to Mother about Pyungsoo since the dinner a few days ago.

Pyungsoo came out of the examination room with his arm in a sling made of a white cloth.

"Dr. Pae said that my arm will still be weak for a few more days."

I could see that the arm was thinner and whiter than the other one. Grandmother thanked Dr. Pae over and over before leaving. Outside, Grandmother crossed the street to the general store. At the store she had the owner pick the best brown pears.

"Where are we going, Grandmother?" I asked. I was sure that she wasn't buying those expensive out-of-season pears for us.

Grandmother ignored me and handed a bill to the man.

"Are we visiting someone?" I asked again.

"We are visiting the Kims." She was annoyed.

"The Kims?"

"It's time," Grandmother explained. "They should see Pyungsoo without his cast."

"Does Mother . . . ?" I didn't finish the question because I knew Mother didn't know.

Pyungsoo glanced at me and tried to hold my hand again.

I hoped when the Kims saw how thin and white Pyungsoo's arm was they might change their minds. After all, Grandmother said that no one wanted to adopt a child with the slightest defect.

We followed her up the hill, then turned right where a row of houses sat on an incline and could be reached by the wide stone steps. Grandmother stopped at the one with roses hanging over the barbed wire on top of the wall. She checked our appearance and fixed Pyung-soo's collar before ringing the bell.

"Who is it?" someone asked from inside.

"Changhee's Grandmother."

An old helper opened the door and bowed to Grand-mother, then ran inside to announce us. Mrs. Kim came and bowed, then received the bag of pears Grandmother handed to her.

"These won't be very sweet," Grandmother said.

Mrs. Kim peered through the opening of the bag. "Our very first this year," she cooed, smiling with her small eyes. "Come in, come in." She led the way to the living area.

"I was hoping your husband was here. How did the talk go with him?" Grandmother asked when we sat down.

"He is surer about him now." Mrs. Kim looked at Pyungsoo in the same way someone would at a puppy.

"Should he see Pyungsoo first?" Grandmother asked.

"No, he is convinced, I think. He said he is getting old . . . and would like to have the boy. He is sure that I would know if the boy is good for us. Besides, he will meet him soon enough."

Grandmother smiled and nodded approvingly.

"Dr. Pae said the sling can come off in about a week. He is ready, I think. Aren't you ready to start a new life?" Grandmother turned to Pyungsoo.

Pyungsoo didn't say anything.

"Then why doesn't he stay here? We could go pick up his things tomorrow. I prepared everything." Mrs. Kim looked at Pyungsoo again before continuing. "I didn't know when he'd be here for certain, but school starts in a week. I got him notebooks, pencils, and even clothes. We do need to go and measure for the uniform."

"The children didn't have a chance to say good-bye." Grandmother glanced at me. I turned my head.

"He could say good-bye when he visits tomorrow."

Then Mrs. Kim said to Pyungsoo, "Do you want to look at your room?" He nodded enthusiastically.

We followed her upstairs in her Western-style house. Pyungsoo's room looked like a room advertised in a children's magazine. There was a new gray metal desk, a clothing cabinet, a bookcase filled with books, and a painted wooden box filled with toys. A fire engine truck, a robot, and a train stuck out on top.

"This is my room?" Pyungsoo's eyes lighted up.

"Everything in here is yours," Mrs. Kim said. "Everything."

Pyungsoo went right to the toys, picked them up one by one, and showed them to me. Then he rolled the wheels of a truck on the floor and let the truck dash around the room.

"Maybe we'll leave him here today then," Grandmother said.

"Grandmother," I said politely, "he is supposed to help me with my insect collection."

"You can come over here and we'll help you," Mrs. Kim said, putting her thin arm around his shoulders.

Even more politely, I said, "Grandmother, he is supposed to help me with my art project too."

"He can come over to our house and do it with you," Grandmother said.

"It's not the same. Besides, Mother doesn't know."

Grandmother made her stupid blinking-eye signals at me. Then she smiled sheepishly and said, "Her mother has taken some *chung* toward the boy and I think it's better if I left him here today. It will be easier for her this way."

I was wringing my hands.

"Pyungsoo and I will come in a day or so to pick up his things. You can always come over here and play," Mrs. Kim said.

"Junehee will like that very much," Grandmother answered.

Pyungsoo seemed lost in his toys. Grandmother took my hand and pulled me, but I shook off her hand and ran down to the first floor.

Mrs. Kim had to call Pyungsoo several times before he came to say good-bye. At the front door I bowed to Mrs. Kim but avoided looking at Pyungsoo, who stood leaning on her with his truck. I said nothing when he said, "See you soon."

The door closed. I turned around and ran ahead of Grandmother.

"Junehee, let's walk together. Junehee!" Grandmother called to me. "Listen to me. If you go home like that you'll hurt your mother's feelings. We need to look happy for her. You want your mother to be happy, don't you? Pyungsoo is better off at the Kims."

I covered my ears but could still hear her. "I'll buy you Chinese food for lunch." I didn't stop running until I was home. I stomped up the stairs to our house, pushed the heavy door, which opened easily from my anger, and walked in. Mother stepped out of the kitchen, wiping her hands on her apron.

I went over to her.

"Where is Grandmother?" she asked.

"She's coming," I said, out of breath.

"Where is Pyungsoo?" Mother asked with apprehension.

"At the Kims. Grandmother left him there."

Mother just stood there and wiped her hands over and over until Grandmother came in.

Grandmother too was out of breath. She avoided Mother's eyes and said, "I left Pyungsoo at the Kims. I stopped by and she insisted. I thought it would be easier for all of us." Grandmother shook her *hanbok* skirt, turned away from Mother, and went into her room.

Mother said, "Yes," but was motionless for a while, then she walked slowly to her vegetable garden.

I went to Soonja Uhnni's room and sat there. I hated Grandmother more than the time she called me the clumsiest child of all the children she knew, and more than when she didn't let Mother go to Mrs. Park's boutique opening. I hated her more than I had for the worst thing she had ever done to all of us.

One day when Mother was out, Grandmother took us to get our hair cut. She said we were just going to get our hair trimmed. When we wanted to wait for Mother, she emphasized that we would be helping her with her workload. Reluctantly we obeyed. Our hair was one of the few things Mother decided, and she let us keep the lengths we liked. Before we went into the beauty salon, Grandmother gave Changhee Uhnni and me money to go buy some "eyeball" candies while we waited for Moonhee and Keehee to get their cuts first.

We thought this was strange because Grandmother hardly ever gave us money for goodies like that. When we returned, Moonhee and Keehee had ugly upside-down bowl cuts. Moonhee kept feeling her hair, ready to burst out crying, and Keehee pulled at her hair. Changhee Uhnni and I protested and said we didn't want our hair cut, but Grandmother coaxed us saying the stylists had made a mistake and this time they would just trim our hair.

The stylists turned us away from the mirrors and bent our heads down and cut quickly. I felt the cold scissors touching my neck but I told myself Grandmother wouldn't lie to us. Our haircuts weren't as ugly as Moonhee's and Keehee's, but they were much shorter than a trim.

On the way home Moonhee cried while Grandmother lectured us about how it was the most economical haircut and how much soap we would save. She said we would thank her later for such easy-to-manage hair.

When Mother came home, Grandmother in her innocent voice told her she had decided that we needed haircuts. Mother didn't say anything to her. She just looked at our hair and said bitterly, "I wanted them to have long hair, but what I want . . . I guess I don't matter." She took crying Moonhee on her lap and gently rocked her and cried with her. For days I imagined Grandmother making a stupid eye signal to the hairstylists behind our backs to make them give us a short cut.

Moonhee came into Soonja Uhnni's room.

"Uhnni, where is Pyungsoo Opa?"

"At the Kims," I said.

"He is not coming back?"

"No."

Moonhee held my hand. "I knew he would be gone

one day. I'm not sad. Are you sad?" she asked in her soft voice.

I shook my head. I was too angry to be sad.

"Mother is going to be sad," Moonhee sighed. "Do you want to make a paper rose for Mother?" On last Mother's Day, I let Moonhee help me make a paper rose that Mother wore until it was torn.

"Devil Granny did it again," I said under my breath.

"Uhnni! You are not supposed to say things like that."

"I'm going to push her off the steps."

"Uhnni!"

"She planned everything. Just like that time when she made us get that haircut."

We heard her footsteps, and the door slid open and Grandmother peeked in. "Everyone else had lunch. Let's eat," she said in her coaxing voice.

"I'm not hungry," I said.

"This was the best thing for your mother," Grandmother answered.

"Grandmother, you planned it this way." I stared at her meanly.

"It's the best way."

"Devil Granny," I said under my breath.

She just stared at me. "Only bad boys like Sungjin say that."

"Devil Granny," I said again, this time a little louder.

"Junehee!" Grandmother raised her voice.

"Mean Granny."

"Junehee!" she shouted.

I heard Mother's footsteps approaching. Without peering in she said, "Apologize." But I said nothing.

"Changhee's Mother," Grandmother said as she turned to Mother, "I thought this was the best way for you, for all of us." Mother didn't say anything but lowered her head, and Grandmother walked away.

Mother came into the room, and I was sure she was going to scold me severely, but Mother just plopped down on the floor, leaned her head against her hands, and closed her eyes.

"I'm sorry, Mother. I won't do it again. I'm really sorry," I said.

Mother brought her apron up to her face with both hands and sobbed into it. Her whole body shook. I had never seen Mother cry so much as that summer. Moonhee slid over to her.

"*Nachom.*" Mother used Father's expression. "Don't I have any feelings? Aren't daughters-in-law human beings? Are my feelings her feelings? Does she know what's best for me? Sixteen years in this household and not once did she know what I felt, not once did she ask me what I wanted, not once did I get to say what I wanted. Do you know what she said to me?"

We just stared at her.

"After three years in this household she said, 'Didn't your mother call you stupid?' because I never said what I thought and never complained. Every day I wiped the table after meals, and every day she pointed, here, there, as if I couldn't see the dirt. Stupid? . . . I guess I am stupid for still being here."

I was getting more and more angry at Grandmother. She sometimes said mean things to people, but I hadn't heard her speak that way to Mother. I did hear her say to Soonja Uhnni once, "You are not so smart. Don't go around saying anything when guests are here. You'll embarrass yourself."

Mother stopped talking. She just sat there wiping her tears with the apron. All I could think of was how Grandmother got me to wear the dressy blouse and good shoes to look presentable to Mrs. Kim. Mother got up, smiled bitterly, straightened her apron, and swept her hair up, then remembered she no longer had long hair and smoothed it down.

"I guess I better go see to her lunch. That's what I'm here for."

After Mother left, Moonhee burst out crying, and I put my arm around her and thought about how much I hated Grandmother. This time I would never speak to her again, ever. And I didn't care if I never saw Pyung-soo again either.

CHAPTER 29

 The Best Thing

A few minutes later, we heard our front door creak and Auntie Yunekyung calling, "Mother, I'm here."

"Mother," she called again, and we heard Grand-mother saying, "I'm in my room."

I heard Grandmother's doors open but there were no words. I guessed Grandmother was silently motioning Auntie to come into her room. Auntie's shoes scraped against the stone step as she took them off, and by the time I peeked, there was no one in the living area.

"You think we should go out, Uhnni?" Moonhee asked me from behind.

I shook my head. I saw Mother come out from the vegetable garden, wash her face by the water pump, and go into the kitchen.

Moonhee and I sat in the room for a while trying to listen to any sound coming from the kitchen or Grand-mother's room.

In front of Mother Grandmother often complained that she hadn't raised Auntie right, and that Auntie didn't have any *chul*—maturity and wisdom. Yet behind Mother's back Grandmother must have told Auntie many things because eventually Auntie knew everything that went on in our house, and she and Grandmother stuck together. The worst thing was, Father ended up agreeing with them. He didn't do it in so many words, but by not saying a thing to help Mother even in small matters.

The previous autumn it was about a *hanbok* Mother wanted to wear. Great-Aunt was celebrating her sixtieth birthday, which was one of the biggest events in one's life beside birth, marriage, and death, and she asked Mother and Auntie to perform a traditional *kochun* dance at the celebration.

Mother knew how to dance well and taught Auntie at our house. We watched Mother moving to the slow rhythm of *tung-tuck-kee, tung-tu-tuck-kee*, and were mesmerized by her ability to move so gracefully. Her arms folded and opened like wings and her legs bent effortlessly to the beat. The white scarf in Mother's hands moved like light and in Auntie's, like paper. Auntie tried to follow Mother's movements but was soon irritated and didn't want to practice anymore.

A few days before the celebration, Great-Aunt sent a violet satin roll for Mother and blue one for Auntie, to have them made into special *hanbok* to dance in. Auntie held Mother's violet satin against her white skin and Grandmother said, "That color is good for you." Auntie looked at herself in the mirror and said, "Yes, this is better on lighter skin. What do you think?" Auntie asked

Father, who was in the room. Grandmother said, "Doesn't that look better on Yunekyung?"

Even though Father knew by the way Mother looked up at him that she liked the violet, he just nodded. Later, Mother said under her breath, "I have no violet *hanbok*. I would have liked one." But Father pretended he didn't hear.

I heard Soonja Uhnni's rubber slippers and the bowls clinking on the lunch tray. She was bringing Grandmother's lunch. Then I heard another pair of shoes and peeked out. Mother with her grocery bag was heading to the front door. I pried my leg gently from under sleeping Moonhee and followed Mother out.

"Mother," I called when she was almost down the stairs. She turned around, but she didn't say I couldn't come. I didn't ask where she was going when we weren't heading to the market, and I didn't hold her hand. Sometimes Mother said it was like holding down her wings.

We walked up the hill toward the mountain that stood guarding our neighborhood. It was strange to be with Mother alone in the afternoon in the mountains. It made me think of places I had seen only once, like the temple in Kyungjoo that was full of strange smells and had a bronze statue of Buddha whose knees were shiny from thousands of touches.

Our shoes were covered with red dirt by the time we came to a flat landing. Under the tall poplar tree with leaves like small hands, Mother folded her market bag for me to sit on, and she sat on her handkerchief. I still had my good clothes on but I didn't sit carefully.

From there we could see our neighborhood stretched below us. The main street divided the area into two, and the side roads branched off into many little ones like a tree. I followed the main street down, counting the side roads from Dr. Pae's large sign, and saw our house. I hoped Moonhee was still sleeping soundly.

A cicada sang above our heads in the poplar branches.

"This family would be better off without me," Mother said, and I held my breath. "After Changhee was born, I thought I couldn't stay here one more minute. I left with her on my back but I saw how sorrowful my child's life would be without a proper home and a father. . . . I could have lived any way, but my children . . ."

Mother spoke to me as if I were a grown-up.

"I thought, I'll stay as long as I can stand it. Sometimes I think one more minute, just one more minute, then I'll go. It's been more than a decade that way."

"Mother—" I started but she interrupted. "Junehee, you are the strongest of the four. Changhee is much like her father, weak inside and stubborn outside. Moonhee, she is obedient but shy and sensitive, and Keehee, she'll grow up to be a little like you." Mother smiled sadly. "You can get along with all of them, can't you? Even with your father?"

Mother looked somewhere beyond our town.

"You'll be the pillar of this family in time." I didn't know exactly what she meant by a "pillar," but I thought I had to act like the son of this family.

Then Mother said bitterly, "You are too much like my side of the family. You'll end up persevering without anyone ever appreciating you. But I'll know. It's hard not to be one of them. We aren't very pretty or well connected, but we are strong."

Mother turned toward me and touched my face gently, in a way that made me glad to be most like her out of the four of us. I was even glad not to take after Grandmother's and Father's good looks. I definitely had Mother's oval face with her high-bridged nose and full lips.

All the relatives called me compassionate, brave, and kind, but no one ever said I was pretty or very smart. The kindest thing they said about my face was that it showed much fortune. One relative, a face reader, said that I had so much fortune that when I got married, I would live without the soles of my shoes ever touching the ground from having so many servants. I didn't believe the part about the servants, but now I believed I was lucky because I was most like my mother.

On the way back, Mother and I bought corn and eggplants at the general store. Then we stopped by a Western bakery and ate pastries with light sweet cream inside. Mother and I loved pastries more than anyone else we knew.

 The Secret

Auntie Yunekyung was still there when we returned, and I felt disappointed. Mother too seemed displeased when she glanced at the red shoes. Moonhee wasn't in Soonja Uhnni's room so I went to mine. When I slid the door open Moonhee was sitting in front of Changhee Uhnni, who had obviously been asking her some questions in her usual bossy manner. Keehee was sitting in the corner, drawing.

"Where did you go?" Changhee Uhnni asked me. "I looked for you."

"Why?"

"What happened in the helper's room?"

"Nothing."

"Moonhee told me you called Grandmother 'Devil Granny.'"

Moonhee looked at me sympathetically.

"So?"

"So, where did you go with Mother?" I didn't think anyone saw us leave.

"To the market."

"For so long?" she asked.

"Yes."

"Where else?"

"Nowhere," I said.

"You are lying."

Changhee Uhnni could sniff out a lie like a cat after a mouse.

"Go look at Mother's market bag. We bought some groceries."

"Where else did you go?"

"Why do you care?"

"I don't care."

But by the way Changhee Uhnni was biting her nails, I knew she wanted to know what happened with Pyungsoo and with Mother. Maybe she was even a little sorry about treating Pyungsoo so poorly. If she wasn't, she would have threatened to take my book reports or better yet, Moonhee's shells or Keehee's drawings, if I didn't tell her. I always gave in whenever she made them cry for something I had done.

"The boy could have stayed here as long as I didn't have to see him," Changhee Uhnni said.

"Too late."

"Where did you go with Mother?"

"I told you, to the market."

Changhee Uhnni gave me her mean sideways glance. "You went to Grandma Min's and to Great-Aunt's and somewhere with Mother."

"You could have gone."

"Not with the stupid boy."

"He's gone. You and Grandmother and Father should be glad."

"I'm glad, so glad that stupid orphan is finally gone." Changhee Uhnni stuck out her tongue and went back to folding a swan from paper. She had done all her summer projects but was working on an extra assignment to get the highest grade.

Moonhee came and sat next to me and mouthed, "Sorry, Uhnni."

There was nothing to do but finish my schoolwork without Pyungsoo. In the wooden box sad and dried-looking insects were pinned to the cardboard back. The cicada Pyungsoo and I found lay between the grasshoppers. I needed more unusual insects, like a praying mantis, a click beetle, a cricket, or more colorful butterflies like the tiger tails, but I didn't know how I was going to find them within a week. He really shouldn't have promised to help me if he was going to leave so easily. He really shouldn't have.

I heard a noise and peeped through the crack of the door, but all I saw was Mother moving in the kitchen. In the garden, a butterfly flew around the last of the pink roses. One day when I look out, there will be straw mats wrapped around the rose stems to protect them from the frost, but winter seemed a long way off just then.

I motioned Moonhee to go outside with me. We left quickly before Changhee Uhnni could ask us questions and went to the storage room to get the net. By the time we got to the rose garden, the butterfly was gone. We searched the vegetable garden but it wasn't there either, so we sat on the steps leading down to the ground and waited. Only a red-tailed dragonfly flew in the sun, showing us the spiderweb design of its wings.

Moonhee and I went to the backyard by the cherry tree to see if there were any insects there. Star rushed out and stood on his hind legs, motioning with his paws for us to come.

Even though Grandmother told us not to, I let Star stand up and lean against me with his paws. When I rubbed his ears and face, he wagged his tail wildly. I filled his empty water bowl and wanted to feed him. Sometimes he didn't get enough food.

"Where are you going?" Moonhee asked.

I put my finger against my lips and quickly tiptoed past the back of Grandmother's room toward the kitchen. The narrow back alley was shaded, and Soonja Uhnni kept the ceramic jars with flat tops containing soybean paste, hot-pepper paste, and some *kimchee* out there. On top of one was a pot of seaweed soup from the night before, and on another, a pot of beef soup bones she was going to reboil for stock. I took a bone and tiptoed back to Star's house. When Star smelled it, he circled around, grabbed it out of my hand, and started to lick it, forgetting all about us.

Moonhee and I went over to the cherry tree. The last of the cherries were shriveled up like raisins, and on the bottom of the leaves were fuzzy caterpillars with orange spots. No one ever brought them for their collection because they were ugly and hard to keep.

On the ground by the tree, I saw an insect wing sticking out from underneath a red brick. Next to it were the remains of the small mounds Pyungsoo had built for his family tombs. Most of the mounds were washed away, and there was nothing on the red brick we had used to hold the food offerings. All I could see was the tattered wing of a cicada that somehow had gotten caught underneath it. I looked up at the sky. Even though the early evening shadows cast the yard in darkness, the sky was bright blue. I wiped my tears before Moonhee saw me, took out the wing and the crushed body of the cicada, and buried it next to the tombs.

We were returning past the back of Grandmother's room when I heard voices. I pulled Moonhee under the high wooden step attached to the outer wall of Grandmother's room. It was damp and spiderwebs hung in the corners under the seat.

"Why are we—" Moonhee saw my face and closed her mouth. We had to be very quiet to hear them, even though the protective wooden shutters were open during summer.

Grandmother's voice was a little muffled. "Let's not talk about this anymore." She sounded like she had a headache.

"Yes, well, don't worry, Mother. I will check." Auntie Yunekyung was excited.

"I told you not to do that. Besides, how are you going to do that?" Grandmother asked.

"If Jungmin Opa has a son somewhere, I will find him. I'll just ask around. I know who his friends are."

"I didn't say he had a son. Your aunt just asked . . . I don't know what is what. He may have . . . but he wouldn't . . ." Grandmother trailed off.

"Don't be so naive, Mother. Look at Father."

"Your father was different. He had women right after we were married."

"It's not just him. It's all of them. Look at mine. He is as good as they come, but do you think he hasn't had a woman outside? I know it. It doesn't mean anything." Auntie added, "What makes you think your son is any different? We need to know whether he has a son."

"He doesn't. Anyway, don't open your mouth about this," Grandmother said.

"Mother! Don't treat me like a child."

"You act like one."

I heard footsteps and quickly led Moonhee around the other side of the house until we were behind my room.

"What is Auntie going to check?" Moonhee asked.

"I don't know."

Moonhee looked at my face closely.

"You do too."

"It's better you don't know."

"I won't tell anyone." She put out her pinkie. "Promise."

"I'll tell you when you are ten."

"That's not until next year."

"I'll tell you then."

"No, please, Uhnni."

"Okay, but you really have to keep quiet. Auntie thinks there may be another boy Mother could adopt." I didn't want to tell her the whole truth. What if Father really had a son somewhere?

"Really?"

"That's what she is going to check."

"That's good, isn't it?" Moonhee asked.

"It's okay. Remember, you promised."

We shook our pinkies.

The dinner table looked very empty without Pyungsoo and Father. Auntie left, saying she had to get back early that evening. Grandmother looked at Mother from time to time and Mother hardly ate, refusing a piece of fish Grandmother put on her bowl. Changhee Uhnni sulked, and I hunched over to hide the prints Star's paws had left on my blouse, but no one seemed to notice them.

 The Giraffe

Breakfast without Pyungsoo was quieter even though he hadn't talked when he ate with us. Father glanced at the spot where Pyungsoo used to sit and went on eating. He had been silent for days, especially after Grandfather's death. Everyone was surprised when he asked us a question.

"When does school start?"

"Next week," I answered.

"All ready for school?"

I nodded even though I hadn't even started my art project.

"Good." He paused. "In one month I'll be going back to America."

"So soon? For how long this time?" Grandmother asked.

"Just for two weeks."

Mother sighed quietly.

"I'm going to need a few underclothes," Father said.

"Yes," Mother answered.

We ate in silence for a while.

"Where do you go at nights, Father?" I found myself asking before I could stop.

"Huh?" He seemed surprised, then dismissed my question by spooning the cold cucumber soup into his mouth. His shiny forehead wrinkled a little and I thought about his father, who he didn't see for over thirty years.

"Where do you go at nights?" I asked again, and heard Grandmother warning, "Junehee."

"You should not be concerned with adult life," Father said, then ignored me.

I stared at his small nose and thin lips. I really didn't look like him.

"Where do you go at nights? I would like to know too." This time it was Mother who spoke up, and Father stopped spooning the soup into his mouth and cucumber pieces slid down to the bowl.

"Huh?" He made his sharp eyes.

"We never see you. The children and I do not see you," Mother said in an even tone.

"What is it you are saying now?" The veins in his temple popped out.

"We would like to know where you are at nights." Mother didn't take her eyes off him.

"You shouldn't involve yourself with men's world. It has nothing to do with you."

"The children don't have a father and I do not have a husband. How could that have nothing to do with us?"

Father just sneered. He finished the few more spoonfuls of rice left in his bowl. Then he cleared his throat and got up and went to his room. Mother walked out after Father. We sat there looking at each other, and Grandmother put down her spoon. It was the first time Mother had ever walked out during a meal.

Father left the house first, then Mother followed with her church books, even though it wasn't Sunday. She returned two hours later and went ahead with her household duties. I watched her all morning but she didn't seem sad or angry. She just worked hard cleaning, organizing, and washing as if we were getting ready to go on a vacation.

At lunch she apologized to Grandmother and Grandmother accepted it, saying she knew how hard it was for Mother to let go of Pyungsoo, and that Father was not being attentive to the family. Grandmother even said she was sorry for bringing Pyungsoo into this family in the first place and causing Mother grief. Mother just sat there and said, "yes, yes," politely.

After lunch Mother reminded me about my art project. I sat with Moonhee and flipped through the book of animals. The year before, I had made a picture book with a story line, but this summer I wanted to sculpt something, maybe an animal that I could hold in my hands. Moonhee liked birds and thought I should make a swallow, but I liked the long neck and pretty eyelashes of a giraffe.

We went to the kitchen with the book. Mother was bent over washing our clothes while Soonja Uhnni swept. Mother rubbed the clothes on the washboard so hard that they made a grating noise.

"Mother, I know what I want to make." She didn't seem to hear me. "Mother?"

"What's that? What do you want to make?" she asked, still rubbing.

"A giraffe." I could see how hard Mother was trying to concentrate by the slight frown under her falling hair. "We can make it out of newspaper. You know, with some glue."

"Then get some newspaper," she said.

"What about the frame?"

Mother asked Soonja Uhnni to get an old fly-swatter that we couldn't use anymore. By the time Mother finished hanging the clothes, we had a pile of newspaper and a swatter. Mother cut through the plastic layer and exposed a long piece of wire underneath. Then she told Soonja Uhnni to make some glue out of cooked rice.

In the pantry/dining room Moonhee and Keehee ripped the papers into thin strips, and Mother and I tried to make the giraffe frame out of the wire. It was too difficult for me, and Mother took the wire, bent it this way and that, and soon it took the right shape.

Moonhee dunked the strips in the watery rice paste and handed them to me. I carefully wrapped the giraffe's head until it began to look real, then the neck, the body, and the legs, each time smoothing over the area until the newspaper gave in to the glue. I shaped the ears by bunching up the paper on each side of its head. For the horns, I took two matchsticks, broke them

in half, and stuck the halves with the red tips next to
the ears.

When I was finished, Mother tilted her head to get a
better look at the giraffe. Then she smoothed it over one
more time. Even though Mother had thick hands, they
moved delicately along the long neck and legs, and the
giraffe became perfect. Mother opened a plastic container and gave me two black beans for the eyes. I
attached the beans to its head with thicker paste, and
our giraffe looked like it was watching us. All that was
left for me to do was to paint it when it dried and attach
some yarn for the tail.

"Mother, do I have to sleep with Grandmother from
now on?" Moonhee asked, rubbing the glue off her
hands. The night before she hadn't been feeling well,
and she didn't sleep with Grandmother even though
Pyungsoo was gone.

"Not if you don't want to," Mother said. "No, not if
you don't want to."

Moonhee smiled uneasily. "If Mother wants me to,
I will."

Mother just shook her head.

That evening Moonhee slept next to me in my room.
She crawled under my blanket and we whispered quietly but got yelled at by Changhee Uhnni anyway. We
waited until she fell asleep.

"Are you going to draw the eyelashes?" Moonhee asked.

"I don't know. Maybe I'll use fake eyelashes, like the
ones Auntie has." I could cut one in half and stick the
pieces on the giraffe.

"She won't give them to you, Uhnni," Moonhee said, yawning.

"You are right." I thought I wouldn't want to ask her anyway.

"When is Auntie going to find this son?" Moonhee whispered.

"Shhh!"

"Sorry," Moonhee said.

"Go to sleep."

"Sorry."

"Okay, go to sleep."

I closed my eyes and listened to Changhee Uhnni's breathing.

The next day was overcast and damp, and my giraffe didn't dry completely, so I couldn't paint it. I did manage to catch a small orange butterfly with black dots and a praying mantis for my insect collection, finishing that project. Mother bought a roll of blue rayon and cut the fabric following patterns she had made from thin rice paper.

Over the buzzing of the sewing machine, I waited to hear the front doorbell ring. Two days had passed but no one had come by the time Mother finished Changhee Uhnni's uniform and started on mine. The small bag I had packed for Pyungsoo with his old clothes, the toy soldier, and the shovel just sat in Mother's cabinet. I suspected that Grandmother had called Mrs. Kim telling her not to come, but I wasn't going to ask her. I wasn't speaking to her.

When Mother was about finished with Moonhee's uniform, we heard the bell. After Soonja Uhnni opened the door, I walked slowly toward it. Mrs. Kim's helper had come, saying she was to pick up Pyungsoo's things because Mrs. Kim wasn't feeling well and couldn't come herself. I looked behind her but I knew there would be no one there.

CHAPTER 32

✺ The Letters

We woke up to the first chilly day. I washed my face and peeked in the kitchen, but I didn't see Mother there. In her room all our uniforms were neatly folded in the corner.

"Where's Mother?" I asked Soonja Uhnni, who was stirring some soup. She didn't answer me right away.

"She's gone."

"Gone? Where?"

"Here." She took out a few envelopes from the kitchen cabinet drawer. "She left this for you."

I took the envelope with my name on it and ran to the vegetable garden. I sat on the step and opened the letter.

My dearest daughter Junehee,
You know how to be good. Take care of the little ones and be Changhee Uhnni's friend. Remember you are the

<p/>

pillar of this family and I count on you. Even if no one else knows how hard you try, Mother knows, remember that.

The door to the garden opened and Moonhee came in with an envelope in her hand. She looked scared and ready to cry. In the letter Mother told her to take care of Keehee and to be brave.

"Uhnni, I should have slept with Grandmother." She broke out in tears. "That's what Mother wanted, wasn't it?"

"She said it was okay, remember?"

"Where is she? Where did she go?"

Soon Changhee Uhnni came and Keehee trailed behind her.

"See? What did I tell you? That boy was trouble. I told you that you'd be sorry. Aren't you sorry now? It was his fault that Mother left. I know it. I told you, you stupid children." She stood on the top of the steps with her hands on her hips, yelling at us. "Mother didn't even say when she was coming back. She may never come back. It's your fault," she said to me.

Keehee came down and sat on the step in front of us.

"Mother is gone?" she asked, and cocked her head. "Gone?"

She handed me her letter and I read it for her, but before I finished it Keehee covered her face like Moonhee and started to cry.

The door opened forcefully, and Changhee Uhnni barely missed getting hit by it. Father stood at the doorway with his legs apart and his hands on his waist. He glared at us for a few seconds with his fiery eyes.

"Stop crying this instant!" he shouted.

But neither Moonhee nor Keehee could stop crying. When Father shouted again, they tried, but they both kept gasping and hiccuping.

"Attention!" We got up slowly and he shouted again. "Attention!"

We lined up at the bottom of the steps.

"If you don't stop crying this instant I'm going to make you stand with your arms in the air. Do you understand?" He glared at us. Everyone nodded except me. "Your mother has gone to see someone and she will be back. There is absolutely nothing wrong."

When Father lied, his eyes became smaller, and his lips, thinner.

He came down the steps and snatched the letters from Changhee Uhnni and Keehee. Moonhee handed him hers. He came toward me and I stepped back. I held the letter behind me.

"Give it to me," he said. I didn't move. "Give it to me now." Father stepped forward and put his hand out. I just stared at him as meanly as I could. "Give it to me!" he shouted at the top of his lungs. "Now."

"It's my letter!" I shouted back.

I saw his hand flying across my face and felt the sting.

"Are you going to give it to me or not?" He put out his hand again.

"It's my letter, my letter, Mother wrote to me!"

He slapped me hard again on the head.

"You made Mother leave! You are a bad man. You and

Grandmother made her leave," I screamed, then my legs buckled and I fell onto the ground.

Father bent down and tried to force open my hand, then ripped the letter out piece by piece. I kicked without looking and wailed, "You made her leave. You and all those other women!"

Father's motion stopped completely. Then he stood up slowly. "What?"

"You and all those other women . . ." I said, crying. "You . . . you made her leave."

He stared hard at me for a long time. Then he turned to Changhee Uhnni and said, "Wash her," and left.

I lay on the dirt crying, and Moonhee came to me and stroked my head.

"Don't cry, Uhnni," she said while crying herself.

I still had a small piece of the letter in my palm.

Soonja Uhnni came in and told us to go and wash our faces. Things were bad enough as it was, she said. We shouldn't make any more trouble. Then she set up a breakfast table for us in the pantry/dining room, but none of us ate.

All day the house was quiet. Grandmother didn't talk to us and pretended nothing was wrong, but went ahead with her routine chore of watering the geraniums, then sang her hymns. I hated the rotten perfumy smell of geraniums and the way she sang the same hymn all the time.

Moonhee and Keehee stayed in the corner of the big room, drawing, and Changhee Uhnni and I sat in my room and tried to read. Earlier Soonja Uhnni had found our letters in the garbage and retrieved them for us, and from time to time Changhee Uhnni took out Mother's letter from between the pages of the book and stared at it. Mine was in so many pieces that it took me a while to tape them all. Though I knew the letter by heart, I read it over many times.

When I felt a little better, I painted the giraffe. I wanted to finish it for when Mother returned. The body and the head were painted brown, yellow, and gold, the horns were painted dark brown to cover the red tips of the matches, and yarn was attached as a tail. Keehee and Moonhee sat with me and kept me company. Through it all, with every little noise we lifted our heads and listened like Star.

All that was left for me to do was paint the giraffe's eyelashes. I ran out to buy a very thin brush, but when I came back from the store, my giraffe was gone from the pantry/dining room. First I asked Soonja Uhnni, but she shook her head. Then I looked in Mother's room and Keehee said she didn't see it. I went to my room and it wasn't there, so I walked around the house looking for Moonhee. As I approached Star's house, I heard Changhee Uhnni's voice.

"You better tell me. I'm warning you. I'm going to drop it."

"Please, Uhnni." Moonhee sounded desperate.

"Then tell me, what son?" Changhee Uhnni demanded.

I came around the corner and saw Changhee Uhnni holding my giraffe. She was poking Moonhee with its head.

"Give me my giraffe," I said, gritting my teeth.

"No."

"Give me my giraffe," I said again slowly.

"You tell me what son Auntie is looking for."

Moonhee stared at me in panic.

"I just told Moonhee that so she could forget about Pyungsoo."

"You are lying. You thought I was asleep. You don't think I heard you. I hear everything. I also heard you the night when Mother came in. What son is Auntie looking for? If you don't tell me . . ." She raised my giraffe over her head and threatened.

"If you break my giraffe, I'm going to destroy your match house," I said calmly. I wasn't scared of her anymore.

"What? No, you wouldn't," she said confidently.

"You want to see?"

Changhee Uhnni let the giraffe slip out of her hand. It hit the ground on one of its hind legs first and then bounced on its side. One leg and an ear broke off and the eyes fell out. I felt my cheeks getting hot. I turned around and ran to our room. Changhee Uhnni quickly ran after me, but I already had the match house in my hand.

"Give me that!" she demanded.

"No, you broke my giraffe."

"Give me that!" Changhee Uhnni screamed at me.

"No."

"If you don't, I'm going to tell Mother about your math test, the time you and Sungjin read the stupid comic books, and playing flower cards."

"Go ahead."

She glared at me.

"You are clumsy." Changhee Uhnni knew how much I hated to be called that.

"Stingy," I yelled back.

"Ugly," she hissed.

"Dark." She hated her dark skin that was like Father's. "You are just like Father."

"I'm not."

"You are just like Father and Grandmother."

"Am not."

"Yes, you are. You are mean, and you hurt Mother all the time, just like them."

"I do not."

"Mother hates you!" I spat out.

Changhee Uhnni stared at me, and her lips began to tremble and tears welled in her eyes. She raised her hand and I stepped back. I thought she was going to hit me. Instead she brought her hand to her face and started to cry out loud, muttering, "I'm not like them, I'm not like them."

I had never seen her cry because of something I had said.

"Everybody tells me I'm like them. I'm not like them." She knelt on the floor and sobbed.

I put down her match house on the table.

I should not have told my sister that Mother hated her. It was the meanest thing I could ever have said.

CHAPTER 33

The Silver Pendant

I waited by the bus stop, feeling for the money I had left from Great-Aunt's gift after I had paid Soonja Uhnni. Standing there at the end of the main street, where it intersected with the major traffic road, I looked for the bus to Grandma Min's house. I knew it should say "Youngdungpo-ku, Daerim-dong" in the front of the bus.

Before sneaking out, I had left a note in Moonhee's bookbag saying I went to Grandma Min's house to look for Mother. Moonhee put all her things back in the bookbag every night, and if I was not home by then, she would see it. Meanwhile, I didn't want her to have to lie for me to Grandmother or Father.

An old woman standing next to me asked if I was alone, and when I nodded she clucked her tongue as if I were an orphan. "Where is your mother?" she asked, and I just smiled. She shook her head disapprovingly. When the right bus arrived, I jumped on it and gave the money to the bus cashier.

"This bus goes to Daerim-dong?" I asked her.

"Can't you see the sign?" she snapped at me as she returned the change.

I found a good seat by the window in the front. I wasn't scared at first but when the bus started to move, I imagined getting lost somewhere and not being able to find my way home. This was the first time I took the bus by myself. I kept saying to myself, "All I have to do is get off at the stop by the market and walk up to Grandma's house, and I will find Mother there."

I recognized the main street that I had seen with Pyungsoo not too long ago. He really shouldn't have left so easily. At least he should have come with his helper and said a proper good-bye to Mother. The next time we meet, I thought, I will just ignore him.

After half an hour, I paid attention to the cashier's words when she shouted out the stops, but she said them so fast I could hardly understand. I started to get nervous. I knew she would yell at me again if I asked her a question.

"Are you alone?" A friendly woman came and sat next to me at one of the stops.

I nodded.

"Where is your mother?"

"At my maternal grandmother's," I answered because she seemed kind.

"Is that where you are going?"

I nodded.

"Where does she live?" she asked.

"Daerim-dong."

"I'm going one stop beyond that. I'll tell you where to get off." She smiled.

Even though I didn't want her to think Mother wasn't a good mother, who made an eleven-year-old daughter ride the bus alone, I was relieved that she was going to tell me where to get off.

"Next stop is yours," the woman said, and I got out of my seat and waited by the door.

"Let her out first," the woman said to the cashier, who stood by the door chewing gum loudly.

I walked down the tall steps to the street level, and there was the market where Mother had bought fruit the last time. I bought a few golden pears for Mother for a hundred won.

From that stop on, everything was familiar—up the hill, turn to the right, then to the left, and there was Grandma Min's. I was out of breath from walking very fast and from the thought of finding Mother. The door wasn't locked and I pushed it. Mother was crouched over by the outside faucet, washing something. She had the water running, so she didn't hear me approach.

"Mother," I gasped.

"Junehee!" She got up, then checked to see if I was alone. "How did you get here?" She wiped her wet hands on the towel hanging on the laundry line.

"I took the bus."

"By yourself? You did?" She was very surprised. "You are too young to take the bus by yourself."

"No, I'm not. See? I'm here." I handed her the pears.

Mother took them and said, "Maybe you aren't too young." Then with a relieved smile, she hugged me.

Her face was thinner since the last time I saw her, and

she had dark lines under her eyes. Mother looked at me closely and touched my face gently. "What happened?"

"Nothing." I covered my face where Father had hit me. There were many little red dots.

"Did Father do this to you?" I didn't answer, and Mother didn't ask anymore. She just took my hand and we went inside.

"When are you coming home?" I asked.

"Not yet."

"Then when?"

"When I've cleared my head."

"How long is that going to take?"

"I don't know."

There was silence.

"Did you finish the giraffe?" Mother asked.

I shook my head.

"School is in a few days. How is Changhee? And the rest?"

"Fine. Aren't you going to come home before school starts?"

"I don't know."

"Can I stay here with you until then?"

"Who knows you came here?"

"No one. I didn't tell anyone."

"Then they'll be worried."

"No, they won't. Can I stay here with you?"

Mother shook her head and smiled sadly. "You have to go home."

"When?"

"Today."

"Today?"

"In a little while."

"Why?"

"Junehee, be a good girl. I need this time," she said gently.

"I don't want to go home."

"I know." She smiled sadly.

Mother let me stay for a couple of hours with her. Grandma Min was out and didn't return while I was there. I helped Mother with the laundry and swept the yard. She made me curry rice, which was one of my favorites, and we ate the pears I bought. We didn't say much the whole time, but I will always remember that day.

I will remember the bus ride, the water-lily pattern on the brown lacquer table, the tartness of the unripened pear, and Mother's hand with new purple tooth marks. But most of all, I will remember her eyes. They were sad and calming at the same time, like the eyes of a deer.

When it came time for me to go, she rummaged through her small bag with prayer books and her rosary and fished out a silver pendant with a Virgin Mary relief.

"Here, you hold on to this. My mother gave it to me a long time ago. You hold on to it." She attached it inside my pocket with a safety pin. I lost things easily.

"I can't stay here with you?" I asked one more time, and Mother shook her head.

I left seven hundred won between the pages of her prayer book while she was in the kitchen. At the bus stop, she gave me a hundred won and told the cashier to make sure I got off at our neighborhood. I sat on the sticky vinyl seat and looked out the window until I couldn't see her anymore.

I pushed our front door quietly. It was near dinnertime but no one seem to have missed me except Moonhee, who ran to me.

"Where were you, Uhnni? I looked for you."

"Where is Grandmother?"

"She went out."

"Does she know I was out?"

"No. Where were you?"

"Out," I said.

"Out where? You were gone for a long time."

I didn't want to tell her where I was. She would be sad and she would have to lie about it if anyone asked. She was a bad liar.

"I went up to the mountain."

"For so long?"

"I needed to clear my head."

Then I took out a candy I had bought for her on the way home from the bus stop, which made her happy. Later, when she wasn't in the room, I pulled out the note from her bookbag and threw it away.

All evening I felt the silver pendant in my pocket. I knew the exact shape of the Virgin Mary with my thumb.

CHAPTER 34

 Mother's Absence

The whole house seemed empty. It didn't feel like just one person was missing but that all of us were hardly there. We did everything quietly and whispered most of the time. The meals we ate together with Grandmother and Father were awkward. Instead of Mother, Grandmother poured the barley tea and served a second helping of rice for Father.

I was sure that Grandmother and Father blamed me for Mother's absence. Neither one spoke to me, and I didn't speak to them. They spent time together in Grandmother's room, talking and sometimes raising their voices. We heard Father shout a couple of times and Grandmother shout once.

Changhee Uhnni wasn't speaking to me after the giraffe incident either, but she wasn't being her usual mean self. She stayed in our room and read books and more books.

I didn't bother putting the giraffe back together. We needed rubber cement and I didn't want to go to Mr. Moon's stationery shop. I couldn't lose myself in books like Changhee Uhnni, or in the little projects Moonhee and Keehee made up for themselves, like finding all the matching buttons in Mother's sewing basket and stringing them together. I went to the vegetable garden, then around the back of the house to talk with Star, out to the front yard, and then to my room.

When I got really restless, I went to Mother's room. I opened her makeup bureau drawers and smelled her handkerchief, and then took out the photo albums from the cabinet and leafed through one and then another. After that, I walked around the room dragging my hands across the mother-of-pearl deer and tree designs on the lacquered cabinet.

On the floor next to Father's ashtray, there were army instruction books. I opened one and it was full of words I didn't understand and many graphs. Then, in the middle where the pages opened easily, I saw an envelope with Mother's handwriting. I took out the letter and opened it.

It's been a long time since I held a pen to write you, almost 15 years. Then, there was nothing I would not have done for you, but now everything is different. I know you think life is difficult for you. But have you wondered how it has been for me lately? I can live knowing about many things, even about your activities outside home. But I cannot live here in this prison if you are not at least a father to our children, and if you do not acknowledge me as your wife. I only expect some respect, not love. Love I know you do not have to give, maybe you never did. I could not go on one more step the way things are, not one more step.

I folded the letter back and put it exactly as it was. It really wasn't our fault that Mother left.

On Sunday, the day before school started, we got ready to go to church without Mother. We put on our good clothes, and Soonja Uhnni brushed our hair and put on our ribbons. The way she was so quiet while dressing us up, even she seemed to miss Mother. Grandmother had already left for her church service, and Father was sitting in the living area making a lot of noise with his newspaper.

When we were almost ready, he got up quickly, changed his clothes, and followed us out.

"I'm going with you," he said, taking Keehee's hand. We looked at each other, then followed him. He didn't say anything more to us.

In church Father crossed himself awkwardly and didn't know the order of the Mass. He followed us one step behind, standing after we stood and kneeling after we knelt. When the Mass was over, we didn't stop by to talk to Father Cho. We followed our father and got in the taxi that he hailed. He instructed the driver to go to Daerim-dong.

Moonhee smiled and squeezed my hand. "Is Mother there?" she asked quietly, and I nodded.

I held Moonhee's hand and she held Keehee's hand. Keehee had not whined or complained since Mother left. But she smiled, showing both her dimples, and I could see how relieved and happy she was now. Chang-hee Uhnni too seemed happy; she didn't push me forward so she could sit comfortably. She just sat at the edge of the seat and looked out the window.

After a long silence, Father cleared his throat and said from the front seat, "Listen carefully," without turning around. "Your mother, she is a good person, a good mother. If you could be half as good as her, I would be satisfied, proud."

We didn't know our father admired our mother.

Father continued, "She knows things that are good for you. You should always obey her. I'm . . . not a good father, do you understand? I'm not even a good person. Do you understand?"

"Yes, Father," we answered.

"Good," he said.

When we got to Daerim-dong, Father told the driver where to go and soon we were in front of Grandma Min's house. I couldn't get out of the taxi fast enough.

"Mother! Mother!" I yelled out as I pushed the door. "We are here."

Even though she didn't smile at Father, the way Mother smoothed her hair made me think she was pleased to see him. She hugged us and led us in, holding Keehee in one arm and Moonhee's hand with the other. Father followed behind us.

We sat with Grandma in the living area while Mother and Father spoke in the other room. She brought us snacks and we ate quietly, waiting for them.

"Your mother said you were first in your class,"

Grandma said to Changhee Uhnni, who smiled and nodded. "That's my granddaughter." Grandma patted her back. "You'll be good to your mother, won't you?" She asked, and Changhee Uhnni nodded eagerly.

"And you, my third granddaughter," she said to Moonhee. "When are you going to get your teeth back?"

"I don't know. They won't come out, Grandma," Moonhee said. "Maybe they will never come out."

"They will, soon. You'll see," Grandma said confidently.

Keehee stretched out her arms, wanting to be held, and Grandma picked her up. "You are not a baby anymore, are you?" Then she gave her a hug.

Grandma looked at me with a knowing smile. "You are ready for school?" I nodded. "You are almost a grown-up, aren't you?" I smiled and she said, "You are."

Mother and Father weren't in the room for long before Father came out and stood outside, smoking his cigarette while Mother packed her bag. When Mother was ready, Grandma gave us some zucchini, cucumbers, and tomatoes to take with us. She followed us to the main street and told us to come by again. Father bowed to her and she shook Father's hand, which embarrassed him and made him bow one more time. Mother squeezed Grandma's hand hard before getting in the taxi.

On the way home, Father told the driver to stop at a restaurant, and we ate dumplings until our stomachs were full. Father didn't watch us too carefully, and he offered dumplings to Mother, who took them even though she was full, like us. Afterward Mother said a pastry would be very delicious, and we stopped by a bakery, ate some, and bought a box of bean cakes to bring home. When we arrived home, Mother carried sleeping Keehee and Father carried Mother's bag. Grandmother winced when she saw us.

Mother bowed and said, "Yes, I'm back," and went to her room to tuck Keehee in. After offering the bean cakes to Grandmother, Father followed Mother in.

When our school started the next day, the weather already hinted of ripened ginkgo berries and colorful leaves. I carried my giraffe carefully, along with the insect collection and the book reports. Mother had helped me glue together the broken parts and my giraffe look as good as new. Changhee Uhnni carried her match house and other projects and walked ahead of Moonhee and me.

The new uniforms Mother made us fit well. They looked better than the ones from the school store. After the long summer, I was glad to see my friends. We looked over each other's summer projects and tried to guess which one would win first prize and be displayed in the school lobby. In class we talked about what we did over the summer. Some went away on a vacation as we did, and others just stayed home, but no one had a stranger come into their family and then leave.

Even if I told myself not to look for Pyungsoo in school, I couldn't help it. He wasn't in my class and for the first two days I didn't see him, but on the third day, as the classes went down to the playground after lunch, I saw his head below me in the staircase. I recognized his big ears, but when he turned to go out, he looked very different. His face had grown round and his uniform of white shirt and blue shorts made him seem like just one of the boys. He had no sling and his arm moved freely. "Pyungsoo," I called, and he stopped and looked up. I saw his shy grin break out, then his mouth stretched wider, showing me a smile I had never seen on his face before.

Epilogue

When late autumn came upon us that year, the rainy season that splattered mud on our feet and the boy who had come into our family were almost forgotten. Everyone was busy making enough *kimchee* to last us a whole winter—a seasonal *kimchee* we called *kimchang*. By early November, cabbages, turnips, and scallions were piled high on the streets, and garlic and red pepper hung in the shops. Mother and Grandmother shopped for the best cabbages and turnips, then had a man deliver them in a rickshaw. The whole house smelled of garlic and raw turnip.

Grandmother called Auntie Yunekyung and Grandmother Boksoon to help us. Auntie sang and entertained us while she worked, and Grandmother Boksoon talked about how happy Pyungsoo was and how fortunate she was to know a family like ours. When all the washing and cutting and chopping was done, Mother and Auntie mixed in the ingredients and went around the yard with their hands full of red peppers. The adults kept tasting the spicy *kimchee* to make sure it had just the right amount of seasoning, especially the hot-pepper powder, then added some more.

When all was finished, Grandmother called one of her church friends, a strong man, to dig the ground. Giant clay pots were lowered into the holes, and the seasoned *kimchee* was put into them to be marinated slowly throughout the winter. Of all the *kimchee*, the *kimchang kimchee* was the best.

By then I was talking to Grandmother again. I began after my birthday in September. Grandmother gave Mother some money so I could have a birthday party, and after that it was hard not to talk to her. She even invited Pyungsoo to the party. He came with a present, which I could tell Mrs. Kim had bought because it was a doll with long hair. When Pyungsoo bowed to Mother, she patted his head and asked him how he liked school, and just for a second, I thought she looked at him longingly. But soon she was off to the kitchen to bring out the food. Pyungsoo didn't stay very long. Mrs. Kim sent her helper to pick him up.

I did see Pyungsoo from time to time in school. He avoided me when he was with his friends, and I pretended I didn't see him. But one clear winter day we were both by ourselves, and he came over and walked home with me. When we were near my house, he stopped and took out the toy soldier from his pocket and showed it to me. The little soldier had lost an arm

and the tip of his nose was broken, but I remembered
how it looked floating on that puddle in the rain.

When Father returned from his American trip, he began
studying a map of that country. He said in three years he
would have been in the army for twenty years, and he
wanted to retire and go to America and start a business.
But three years was a long time. That was three *changma*
away, and I still worried and waited for our auntie to
walk in one day with a stranger and say, "Here, here is
the son."